The Man Who Lives in Dream

Sarathi Sabyasachi Sahoo

Email:
sarathisahoo@gmail.com

This novel is entirely a work of fiction. The names, characters, organizations and incidents portrayed in it are the work of the author's imagination. Any resemblance to actual persons, living or dead, events or localities, is entirely coincidental.

The views expressed in this book are entirely those of the author. The printer/publisher, and distributors of this book are not in any way responsible for the views expressed by the author in this book. All disputes are subject to arbitration; legal actions if any are subject to the jurisdictions of courts of Kolkata, India.

ISBN: 978-93-84333-67-6

First Published: September 2014

Price: ₹230/-

Cover Design
Abira Das

Distributed by
purushottam-bookstore.com
power-publishers.com
flipkart.com
infibeam.com
crossword.in
amazon.in
ebay.in

September 17th, 2071.

I was sitting in my garden enjoying my morning coffee, with a customary *T-Paper* - an electronic paper by the Trimage media conglomerate – in my hands, when a piercing shout broke the serenity of it all.

"Dad, uncle Rohit's on the phone. It's urgent!"

"Rohit...? Huh... After all these years, the idiot finally had the decency to call once!"

I ran into the house and hastily grabbed the phone.

"Hello, Rohit. It's been a really long time. Fighting with the wife again?!" I quipped with a smirk on my face.

"Oh, come on..." Rohit dismissed from the other side. "This isn't the time to joke, man. Go put on *Live Today*, now!"

"Why? What happened? I was just reading *T-Paper*. I didn't see anything big."

"This is breaking right now, they probably missed it. Listen, just put on Live Today, all right?!" a worked-up Rohit hung up the phone.

"Jolly, please switch on the TV to *Live Today*." I asked my daughter.

"TV, turn to *Live Today*, set volume at 60." she gave the voice command.

(Television) World president Rosu Minter addresses a press conference, "Today is a black day for the whole world. A few moments ago we received shocking news from the Sanjivani Hospital that the 'God of Peace', Sir Amit Khanna, passed away

early this morning. Just two short years ago we celebrated him being the only person to have been awarded the 'Golden Novel' prize, the greatest and most prestigious honour in literature. With a heavy heart, today I declare a worldwide vigil of silence for one minute commencing at 12:00hrs GMT."

In a state of shock, I slumped down on the sofa with my hands over my mouth. Old memories suddenly flashed before my eyes. Utterly speechless, a torrent of images from a bygone era crossed my mind again and again.

This isn't about me or my family. This is a story about two friends, Amit Khanna and Amit Saraf.

July 28th, 2052.

I had just graduated that year. I and some of my friends from college went to picnic on a beach somewhere in the outskirts of Mumbai. Not Juhu or its ilk, one of the lesser known ones where there wouldn't be tourists. We planned to leave by evening but the unpredictable weather summarily thwarted that. It was still monsoon, we should've known better. At dusk the sky darkened pretty quickly and gusts of winds blew sand in our faces. A storm was coming. We ran towards the surrounding jungle just as it began to rain. Within a few minutes it started raining so heavily that visibility was almost zero. We stayed together without panicking. We went deeper inside the jungle hoping to find some shelter until we finally landed on a small old cottage. A decrepit sign-board said "Private property. No trespassing." But it was raining too heavily to obey trespassing laws, and made our way till we reached the rusty lock outside.

"Is there anything we have that we can break this?" I asked.

"Hey! This may be someone's cottage. It's illegal to break the lock." Karthik objected.

"Oh, come on. If we don't break the law now then all of us might die of pneumonia. We can face all the fines and punishment later, but for that we need to save our lives first."

"Yeah, I have a toolkit in my bag." Rohit unfastens his backpack. "May be it will work."

"Cool, give me that." I waded through the bag as Karthik nodded apprehensively.

Atif and Sudheer watched our backs as we started picking the lock.

We finally broke in. Nobody had been inside for decades it seemed, the wooden room was filled with cobwebs and a thick layer of dust coated everything. There were no furniture except for a rack full of books and a small bed with a dirty mattress. Anyway, we finally had a roof over our heads to save us from rain. We lit the room with our flashlight and had some wine and baked bun that was leftover from the picnic.

Karthik and Sudheer started playing on their portable gaming device. I was getting a little bored after sometime. I prayed for the rain to stop but it wasn't listening to anybody other than the sky that sent it. As my eyes darted around the room they got stuck on a big diary kept on the book shelf. I wondered who had still been writing on a paper diary in this digital era.

"Hey guys look what I found - An authentic handwritten diary." With much curiosity I picked it up.

"Oh, great! Let me see. My dad used to maintain a diary in his youth. But I have never seen one yet." Rohit said, peeking over my shoulder.

"Me too...!" Karthik looked up from his gaming device.

"Can we read this?" Sudheer asked, pocketing his device.

"I don't know, it may be a personal diary of somebody. It might have some personal stuff not meant for-"

"Just stop..." Atif interrupted. "You see this cottage? It's been locked for eons. Besides, we don't know the writer. So, it doesn't matter if we get to know some of his secrets."

All of us agreed with Atif and decided to read this. At least we won't be bored in this lonely place.

So I started reading it aloud:

(Inside fold) I'm Amit Khanna. I started this diary from first year of college. When you are reading this if I'm already dead, please bury this beside my grave. That's my only request.

Ages 5 to 17.

I have always had bad dreams since I could remember but I was just a child then. I couldn't tell the difference between that and waking life till I was 5.

I hailed from an ordinary middleclass background with a dad working at a bank and a housewife mom.

"Dear, it's 10 already. Switch that darn thing off. It's bed time." Mom said.

"Mom, I won't sleep tonight. Let me watch TV please!" I replied clutching the remote ever closer.

"What? Don't be stubborn. Shall I call dad? GO TO BED!"

"But mom the ghosts will come for me in my dreams again."

"Oh, those are only dreams dear. Don't worry you'll be here with me."

"I know it's a dream. But I get to know that after I wake up. When I am dreaming, it all seems real and if I'm hurt in the dream I can feel the real pain. Please mom, don't make me go to sleep!"

"What nonsense! If you don't get a good night's rest how you will go to school tomorrow? Dreams can't harm you dear. Now go to bed! I'll be with you here." She switched off the light.

I lay in bed with eyes open. Time passes. The minutes felt like hours. Around 11 I finally close them.

Dream Log:

I was in my house with friends from my colony.

"Let's play hide and seek." Bunty said.

All agreed and made Bunty the "it".

"50, 49, 48...1 and here I come." Bunty shouted.

Everybody found somewhere to hide- inside the closet, behind the door, around the corner - but I couldn't find any place. Finally, I found a store room that had an old bed and I hid under it.

I waited for 15 minutes but nobody came. That's it, I had to go outside. Upon opening the door I saw I was in a different house. I ran outside and saw just this one house. Night had fallen and I didn't know what to do. I shouted "Bunty... Pinku... Shelly..." No reply. I ran back into the house and sat in a corner with my hands trembling and sweating bullets. I started sobbing.

Suddenly there appeared a faint shadow and it kept getting closer and clearer. I started having panic attacks. Just then the power goes off too.

I woke up screaming.

"Hey, calm down. What happened dear?" Mom grabbed me by the shoulders.

I kept murmuring. It was already dawn.

Later that day mom took me to the zoo and I had a great evening.

"Today you got to see flowers, rabbits, elephants, tigers and so many other nice things. You will have good dreams tonight." Mom tried to reassure me.

"Really...?" I was bewildered. "Do you know for sure?"

"Our dreams borrow from what we see in real life. If you see good things, you will dream good things." Mom stroked my head.

That night I lay in bed thinking about the whole day - How I enjoyed at the zoo, had my favourite chocolate ice-cream.

And before I knew it I was back dreaming again.

Dream Log:

I was in the zoo with all my school friends. There were some monkeys in a big cage. They teased us for more when we threw some peanuts inside. We then went to the lion cage. We were all having a blast. Suddenly, everybody disappears. I'm the only one in the zoo. Even the animals are gone.

I just simply started running. I came up to a big gate and when I went outside, I found myself in the jungle. It was so dense I had to stop to see where I was going.

I heard an evil laugh getting closer. I started running again. As I dashed in between the trees I found myself at the mouth of a big waterfall. I had taken a wrong turn. Panting and nowhere to go I jumped yelling at the top of my voice.

I woke up. Sweating and shocked.

As the years went by I got more accustomed to such regular nightmares. I realized that those 8 hours every night would be the worst part of my day for the rest of my life.

June 12th, 2002.

I was staying in the hostel of the engineering college I had joined. I had two roommates - Praveen and Amit. To avoid confusion we called him by his surname Saraf. We became friends pretty fast and began sharing a lot about our lives with each other. When they got to know about my dreams they felt really bad. So bad in fact, that one day Saraf dragged me along to go somewhere, and to my surprise it was a psychologist's clinic. Her name was Sarah, a bespectacled white lady in her thirties with short hair and a tall physique.

"You are Amit, right?" She asked.

I nodded.

"Please, sit down."

I sat on a chair in front of her desk.

"So tell me Amit, Do you recall the first time you had one of these bad dreams?"

"Umm... Don't know exactly. I have been having these since childhood."

"Ok. Did you ever experience any traumatic events in the past? I mean is there any accident you were always thinking about or perhaps an abusive relationship or interaction?" she asked squinting her eyes.

"No Madam, never in real life. Things of that sort happen only in my dreams." I replied.

"Are you afraid of ghosts, spirits or supernatural entities?"

"Not in waking life, no. However, I have encountered plenty of situations in my dreams where I am inclined to such fears. But as soon as I wake I realize it was yet another normal bad dream."

"Meaning it doesn't affect your daily life since you take them as just a bad dream?"

"Yeah... But what about those eight hours of my daily life...?! I feel everything that happens within my dreams. Won't it harm my quality of life even a little bit if I am always afraid to go to the bed, as I know I will lead a horrible existence for the next few hours?"

"So did you try anything to stop such dreams?"

"Absolutely, ever since I was kid. And more so now as understand it a little better. But what can you do really? Ironically enough, dreaming doesn't care about our whims and fancies!" I chuckled.

"Do you remember the worst one you ever had?" She re-crossed her legs.

"Those eight hours every night are all equally bad. In the real world, I find them all so silly but I don't know why they scare me so much when I am back there."

"You use the word 'silly'? This means you know how ridiculous these dreams actually are!"

"Yes, But that realization only dawns on me after I wake up. But when I am dreaming, I can really feel the fear and the adrenaline as if it's real life."

"Why do they seem 'silly' then?"

"I was speaking in terms of logic. Let's say I was walking on a road. Suddenly I find myself running on water and an airplane is about to crash on it. Everything feels real and strikes fear in my heart. If all that's true then why doesn't the lack of logical causality in that string of events also hit me too?! You see what I'm saying?"

"That is strange!" Sarah strokes her chin. "I have had bizarre dreams too but they aren't always bad. Our dreams reference images and memes from our daily lives. But it doesn't present the whole picture with logic as it is the product of our unconscious mind. Hence, logic takes a back seat. That said you look very normal to me. I'm not sure if I can be of any help as there's no presentable abnormal behaviour of your mind that affects your daily life. All I can suggest is perhaps a little yoga every morning for 30 minutes at least. May be it can influence your unconscious mind to stop the repetitive negative patterns."

"Thanks doctor. I guess I will try that too. Goodbye."

Months go by. Yoga did not help at all. After all the bad dreams and occasional ragging, albeit without malice, I moved on to the 2nd year.

September 2nd, 2003.

We were all so excited that day. We will finally be declared as one of the seniors. Everybody in our batch was very curious as to how we would welcome the year's juniors and have our fun with a little ragging. We all discussed about how we would start the ritual hazing in creativity ways.

Before entering through the college gates, we stopped all the juniors and asked them to stand in a queue. We began by asking them to give a formal introduction. All the juniors were so nervous and frightened. Suddenly a girl in a blue suit caught my eyes. She was looking down at the ground glancing up every one in while. I don't know what happened exactly but I kept staring at her. She was beautiful, yes, but not conventionally. Something about her eyes attracted me, snared my unblinking attention. Many introductions later and her turn came. She was trembling with fear.

"Introduce yourself." Naveen said with heaviness.

"I'm Anushka. I'm from—"

"Hmm... Anushka 'who'...? Anushka 'Clinton'?"

There was a cacophony of laughter. She was standing still in the same position. One could smell the fear.

"Did you hear?" Naveen pressed on.

"Sorry sir, I'm Anushka Patel."

"That's it? That's your intro??"

"I'm from Gujarat. And—"

"Are you not from India?"

"Yes sir."

"? Which place? You shit for brains!"

"Ahmedabad, sir."

"So, what is the capital of Ahmedabad?"

"Gujarat, sir."

Everybody laughed even louder.

"Sorry sir. Ahmedabad is the capital of Gujarat!"

She was panicking now.

"Come on guys, look at her. She is totally lost. Let her go." I intervened.

"Next."

"Thank you, sir." She swiftly turned and left.

My eyes were still fixed on her as she briskly walked away. I have always heard about love at first sight but always thought that was relegated to the world of movies. I couldn't reconcile what I felt. Was it love or just another crush? Anyway I forgot about it for the moment. Thought I would let things happen the way they may.

"La... la laa... la la... Laaa..." I hummed along through the rest of the queue.

Later that night I was only thinking about Anushka's face and I don't remember when I fell asleep and started dreaming again.

Dream Log:

I was in class. Niharika madam was taking the software engineering class.

"What are the various models of SDLC?" Madam asked aloud.

Suddenly an alarm went off. Everybody rushed outside.

"What the hell?" I exclaimed.

We were on a big ship floating on the ocean.

I couldn't understand how I came there suddenly. Everybody was running helter-skelter. Through all the bodies I saw Anushka running towards me shouting "run! Run...!"

Upon looking closer outside I found a big iceberg approaching the ship and before we knew it the port side of the ship had a big collision. Out of nowhere I had a Deja vu. I had seen this before somewhere. Where... Where was it? By gosh! Wasn't this Titanic? I took the stairs to the upper deck and read the writing on the plaque. It was the Titanic! What in the world was I doing there? I panicked. It must be a dream! Yes, it was a dream... "Oh come on now. Wake up!" I shouted aloud.

Suddenly I heard, "Amit... Mr. Amit!" I woke up and found myself in class.

"Did you not sleep last night? Is this the place to catch up on your missed sleep?" She frowned. "Stand up! Tell me about the topic we are discussing today."

"Oh, Thank god it was a dream. I promise I won't watch any horror movies before sleeping"

"Mr. Amit! Are you listening? I asked what is it that we are studying today?"

"Sorry Mam, It was a bad dream." I fidgeted with my notebook. "Well you asked 'What are the various model of SDLC?'."

"What? Are you still dreaming? This is a physics class. Not computer!"

I was completely dumbfounded. Before I fell asleep I was in the computer class. And who was this professor? I hadn't seen her before. She wasn't Niharika madam...

"Mam did you join the teaching faculty recently?" The classroom burst out laughing.

"Shut up! Go, get out of the class. Today you'll have an appointment at the dean's office."

"But Mam—"

"Shut up and get lost."

I coolly walked out of the class and went outside to the cafeteria. There I saw Anushka sitting alone having coffee. I became so elated. I went to her table.

"May I?"

"Oh, Yes please!"

She grabbed my hand and started kissing it. I was on cloud nine but couldn't understand what was happening..."

"Let's go somewhere outside of campus."

She dragged me by my hand towards her scooty.

"Sit, I will drive. But it wouldn't be a little funny though- you riding pillion behind a girl?!"

"No, no. I will drive, you sit." I handed her the spare helmet.

I started the ignition and drove towards the college gate. Out of nowhere a big truck hit us and we flew down the road. The truck had crushed Anushka's head and disappeared from the road. Darkness surrounded my eyes. There was blood everywhere. I was crying like a child.

"Oh, God... why...?" I screamed with my bloody hand towards the sky. "Why would you do this to me? The one girl that I ever loved and you had to take her away from me? Please say this is a dream..."

"Yes it is a dream. Wake up Amit. This... Is... a... Dream..." A deep baritone voice surrounded me.

I woke up and found myself in bed, panting and sweating profusely. I never thought I would be this glad realizing that something was just another one of my dreams. But why was Anushka there and in such a bad one at that? I didn't dare sleep the rest of the night. I just sat there all night thinking.

It was really getting too much now. I had to do something about these dreams. That night's was particularly scary. But a strange one at the same time- I had a dream inside a dream. Moreover it was the first time I actually told myself that it was a dream. And that bit really puzzled me. How come I knew it was a dream. I mean I wasn't sure at that time, but I realized that I had specifically instructed myself that it was just a dream and made myself wake up from it. Just then I had a moment of insight - what if I could take a message from the real world inside my dreams. I could make myself aware that it's just a dream and not be afraid. But would that be possible?

The next morning I talked about the dream to Saraf. I described everything I witnessed.

"Saraf, is it possible to communicate with one's dreams?"

"Well, I don't know. But if you try, you can make most things possible. It's all about having the resolve."

"Hmm... I need to try at least. Do you know anyone who might help me with this?"

"No, I don't think so. If you believe in yourself, you can make it happen. Everyone else may question your sanity but fuck them. There is no one but you who can help you. Only you can do it."

Saraf's words gave me a mission in life. From that day on I have always tried to send messages to my dreams. I started writing my own thesis on dreams. I researched all over the internet and gathered as much information as I could. It seemed like I already started leading a second life apart from my studies. I tried to define my dreams and how they came. I learnt about all kind of dreams. I visited the blind and noted how they dream without any visuals. I went to the deaf to note their mute dreams. I started constructing my own theories about dreams.

I spent the rest of my time in college this way till I finished my B.Tech in 2006. During this time I tried courting my love to Anushka but that did not pan out. All of us became close friends over the years. I got a good job in a leading software company. Saraf also joined the same company and both of us moved to Bangalore. We were always discussing about dreams and Saraf always gave me moral support.

August 8ᵗʰ, 2007.

I got a call from my insurance agent.

"Hello sir! How are you doing? I'm waiting at the reception." He said in his usual over-enthusiastic manner.

"Oh, I'll be there in 2 minutes."

"Sir, please don't forget to bring the necessary documents that we discussed earlier."

"Yeah, I have them ready."

I went to the reception and looked around trying to guess what an insurance agent might look like. My eyes caught a person with some files tucked under his arms. I guess that was him.

"Excuse me, are you from 'Future Safe'? ...The insurance company?"

The guy nodded and asked me to sit on the chair beside him.

He handed over some forms and asked me to sign on all the marked pages. While I was going through them, I noticed something. The guy was dragging his shirt collar up frequently. Maybe once a minute.

"Excuse me, Do you feel uncomfortable here?" I asked.

"Why sir...?" He curiously looked at me.

"I noticed every minute you are dragging your collar. So—"

"Oh... Sorry sir... I'm not aware when I do that. It's one of those habits you get from your days in school!"

"Habit huh?! If you don't mind my asking, can you tell me how it started and what you do when you're wearing a shirt without collar? Please don't feel weird. I'm actually doing some research about habits and it will be so helpful if I can get some more information from you."

"Okay. Sure Sir, No problem. Well, in my school days I used to regularly break the top buttons of my shirt. So to avoid showing my bare body I always used to drag my shirt upwards. Ever since that I developed this bad habit. As grew older I tried to stop, but still do it unconsciously. Even if I don't have collar on my shirt, my hands would still go up. But I become aware of it when I inevitably don't find the collar and stop myself." He chuckled.

"Thank you. This might help me later."

I finished all the documentation and went back to my office. I was still thinking about his strange habit. Night had fallen but I was still thinking about it. I took notes for my thesis. I tried to co-relate dreams and habits. Suddenly I felt like I had a breakthrough. If both originate in the unconscious mind then would it be possible for habits to manifest in dreams or vice-versa? I decided to ask the insurance agent.

The morning after, I gave him a call.

"Hello..."

"Hi, this is Amit Khanna. We met yesterday regarding the insurance policy?"

"Oh, yes Mr. Khanna. Tell me what can I do for you?"

"Actually I need to know something more about that habit of yours if you don't mind."

"Of course, sir... No problem... Ask away."

"Do you remember your dreams after you wake up?"

"Umm... sometimes... Why...?"

"Do you remember doing your shirt collar thing in your dreams?"

"Hmm... I never noticed. Maybe or maybe not."

"That means you never saw yourself doing that in your dreams, right?"

"Most Probably... I don't think I ever had a dream like that."

"Okay, thank you very much. May I call you again if I need more information?"

"Anytime, sir..."

"Great! Thanks. Really appreciate it. By the way, I never got your full name—"

"Pradosh Saxena, sir."

"Thank you Pradosh. We will talk later."

I felt a little helpless knowing he probably didn't have his habit in his dreams. Then was it just an external behaviour manifesting only in reality that our conscious mind doesn't know of?

A knock on the door broke my train of thought. It was Saraf.

"Good morning."

"Hey, good morning...!"

"Ready for work...? "

"Saraf, Uh... How about I take a leave today? You can mail to the team that I'm not well   ."

"Sure, but what happened? Is everything fine?"

"Oh, yes. I just need to write something for my thesis. This bit is particularly important."

"What is it that's so urgent?"

"Actually I met someone with a strange habit. I want to investigate about how habits can reach into dreams."

"Hmm... Interesting point... Okay, carry on. I'll send the mail."

After Saraf left I started thinking again but couldn't figure out what to do. Finally, I poured myself some whisky. First peg down, then a second and then another. After the sixth peg I was absolutely lit up.

I started talking to myself. I went to the mirror and gazed into my own eyes.

"Amit, you have to communicate with your dreams. Otherwise you'll waste your whole life having them one bad one after another." A voice inside me chimed in.

"Yes. I'll do it, now I'll go to sleep. I can do it. Today I will talk to my dream."

As I moved towards my bed I tripped on the door mat. Somehow I caught the foot board of the bed and halted my fall. I pulled myself up to the bed and sat down with my back rested on the wood. My eyes were about to close. I was blacking out. I felt so powerless. I closed my eyes and again conversed with myself.

"Amit, today I will come to your dream and help you. Don't worry; I will come for you today. Yes I will come..." The voice reassured me while I dozed off.

Dream Log:

I was in a bar drinking with Saraf. We're already hammered and having a conversation.

"Saraf, this has gone far enough. I should stop dreaming about scary stuff. From now on I'll always go into my dreams and save myself."

"Yes. You'll and I'll too." Saraf patted my back.

"(Laughs) how you will go into my dream?"

"If you can take yourself into your dream, then you can take me too. We both will go and save you."

"Okay. Save for one condition. You'll have to invite me to one of your dreams too."

"You have my word on that. But your turn first. So, when do we go?"

"Tonight, when I fall asleep, I'll go into the dream and then I'll call you. But I'm not sure how we'll actually save Amit."

Saraf put his hand in his jacket and pulled out a pistol.

"See, I have a pistol."

"Whoa, let me check what I have."

I put my hand inside my jacket and found a bomb.

"I have a bomb."

Then Saraf pulled out a rocket launcher from his jacket and I pulled a laser gun. This went on for a while till there were weapons strewn all over the table.

"Hey, we have a lot of weapons. Now we can absolutely save Amit in the dream." I said rubbing my hands in excitement.

"But where did we get all these weapons from?" Saraf asked.

"I have no--" before I could finish a group of rowdy rough looking people rushed towards us and put a gun on my head.

"Who… Who are you? What do you want?" I asked visibly shaken with adrenaline rush having sobered us up.

"You have something that belongs to us." The biggest guy retorts calmly.

"What are you talking about?"

"Tell us where the diamonds are or else."

"But we don't know anything about diamonds!"

After not haring what they wanted to hear they decided to tie us and torture us for answers. One of them jabbed a big needle in my hand.

"Please leave me, I don't know anything about diamonds, I'm just a software engineer." All my screaming fell on deaf ears.

"Then why do you have all these weapons?"

"I don't know man, please leave me. Help! Someone please help me! Someone please save me…"

Suddenly a voice from the sky filled the air "Leave them or I'll destroy all of you" Everybody looked up. In an instant the bar was gone, the thugs had disappeared and Saraf and I were sitting on a beach that stretched for miles.

"Saraf, what was that? Where did those guys go?"

"I don't know. Who cares? Let's get the hell away from this place."

I came around and woke up. Oh God, what was that? That was first time ever that I woke up without getting hurt in a dream. But where did that voice come from? Who was that came to my rescue?

I kept asking myself more questions. It was six in the evening by then. I still had a bad hangover due to the excessive whisky. The doorbell rang. I opened the door and it was Saraf.

"Hey, you look so tired. What happened?" Saraf asked.

"Nothing like that... I just woke up now." With a heavy breath I replied.

"Did you sleep throughout the day?"

"Yes, I took a little too much whisky and slept all day."

"What? Why?! Is that a part of your experiment too?!"

"Well, something like that. Anyway I have something to share."

I told him all about the dream.

"Wow. That is strange but it's also some good news finally. At least there was someone to save you in the dream."

"Yes, but I don't know who that was. And why I couldn't see him. I only heard his voice and then I woke up."

"Hey, you said that before you going to sleep, you were asking yourself to save Amit in the dream, right?"

"Yeah I did. Oh... does that mean, the voice was mine?! Hmm... That is a possibility."

"Great! Still I can't believe you went into your dream to save yourself. *(Laughs)* this time you saved me too!"

"Stop it dude, this is not a joke. Anyway, let me be sure first."

"How can you be sure that was you? Are you going to start drinking excessively before going to sleep from now on?"

"No, that wasn't due to alcohol. It must be that I finally mustered enough willpower."

So what you will do now?

"I will do the same things before sleeping."

"Meaning...?"

"I will make my willpower more even stronger. And before going to sleep I'll make a promise to myself to save Amit in the dream."

"Hmm... Let's see. Anyway, had your lunch today?"

"Nope... Feeling hungry..."

"Ok, get ready. We'll go to a restaurant now and have a little party."

"Party...? Why?"

"Any guesses?"

"Umm..." I shook my head.

"I got a promotion today and also a 50 grand bonus."

"Awesome! Congratulations man. And tomorrow is weekend as well. Let's go and enjoy tonight."

We went to a bar-cum- restaurant. We had a pretty good evening there. I got drunk again and came home around eleven.

"Okay Saraf, I'm going to bed."

"Goodnight. And don't forget to save Amit in the dream."

"Oh yes... Thanks for the reminder. I'll definitely save Amit tonight."

As I lay in bed, I closed my eyes thinking the same.

"Amit, tonight also you won't get into any trouble. I'll save you from anything. I'll save you Amit... Yes, I'll save you... I'll save you..."

I kept promising myself that and never realized when I fell deep asleep.

Dream Log:

I was on a flight with Saraf beside me. He looked excited.

"At last our paper got selected for publication in 'Tech Pulse'." Saraf exclaimed.

"Really…? So are we going to America?" I asked.

Yes, so much hard work finally paid off. I thought about it a little… One day I am writing the paper on my desk, the other day it gets published on the board, then I get a call from the U.S. and now all of a sudden I'm on this airplane."

I looked outside through the window. It was dark with the occasional lightening. I turned towards the aisle. All the passengers were asleep.

"Saraf, I don't know why but I feel something wrong might happen."

"Why you are thinking like that? Tomorrow morning we will be in U.S.A.!"

"Yes, but I have a fear of flying. That's why I always avoid flights and take the train to travel."

"What, you want to go to the U.S. by train?"

"But I have this fear—"

"Relax." Saraf interrupts. "Flying has the least chance of any accident compared to any other mode of travel."

"Everybody says that. In a train at least there is a chance to survive. But up here there is no chance. Not to mention I'm afraid of heights."

"Do one thing - close your eyes and try to sleep till morning."

"What? Never... You know I have bad dreams... And now I'm on a plane. There is no way I'm going to sleep. Do you have any liquor? It might loosen me up a bit."

"It's an international flight buddy. You can get everything. Let me call the airhostess." Saraf pressed a switch.

"Yes sir, how may I help you?"

I turned around and saw a cute lady standing there. She looked awfully familiar.

"Saraf, doesn't she look like Anushka?"

"Yes, she is Anushka."

I looked at her face again. I don't know how but her face totally changed into Anushka's face.

"Anushka, what are you doing here? You are an airhostess?"

"Yes dear."

But I remember her doing computer engineering, how come she went into this profession.

"What about your B.Tech degree?"

She came and sat down on my lap. She started playing with my hair. I was in heaven now. I didn't even want to know how it happened. Without caring a bit I planted a small kiss on her forehead.

"Are you still having bad dreams dear?" Anushka asked.

"Yes." I replied.

"Is not this a dream?"

"No way... My dreams are never this sweet."

I quickly realized something. Yes, it may be a dream.

"Hey Saraf, is this a dream?"

Suddenly, Anushka wasn't there anymore. I looked around frantically. All passengers were still sleeping. Saraf was listening to something on headphones. Then it dawned on me - It was a dream. But it was such a nice one. I wish I could see such dreams every day.

"Saraf, I just had a really nice dream."

"How come...? Did you drink too much again or what?"

I looked down to find an empty glass in my hand.

"Oh, I was drinking then. But what a dream it was!"

Suddenly, I felt a big jerk. The plane started shaking. Some of the passengers started screaming.

"Calm down." Saraf shouted. "It's just a little turbulence outside. It's pretty normal. All the lights go off on the plane."

"(Announcement) we are going through a big turbulence. We'll have to fly on top of it. It needs some more power. So we switched off the lights. Please fasten your seat belts and don't get panic"

The plane kept rattling. I was so frightened at that time. I was praying to God.

"Don't panic. I have seen much more dangerous situations than this on a plane."

"(Announcement) one of the engines are damaged. We are trying to make an emergency landing. Please be seated."

Now everyone started shouting in the plane.

"Fasten your seat belts. Everything will be okay."

I felt that we're falling from the sky. We couldn't do anything. I was screaming at the top of my voice. "Oh God, please help us... Please help us this one time... I promise I'll never travel by air again."

Suddenly the pilot burst through the cabin door and ran up to me. Holding my hands, he said "Nothing will happen, I will save you. Don't cry. See you are in an airport now." I looked all around me and saw that I was in an airport.

"What happened? Why you are shouting?"

"We are on the plane, right?"

"We were. And now we are at airport."

"What about the turbulence?"

"That's over and we have already landed safely."

"Huh..." I couldn't understand anything. "Anyhow, we are safe now. But I'll never travel by air again."

I saw a light coming from the customs and immigration gate and I went into the light.

I woke up. It was a dream. But the ending was so nice. I escaped from the plane crash!

I looked out of the window. After a long time I actually "felt" the morning sunshine rather than it just falling on me. I checked my cell phone for the time, "8:20". I brought my diary over and started remembering the whole dream and noting things down for my thesis. How could a dream be so weird and illogical? How come the pilot ran to me and promised me safety? And just after that I found myself in the airport without a scratch on me! And why was Anushka there in an airhostess uniform... Now that was a really good experience. But how did she disappear in an instant? I asked myself so many questions...

I knocked on Saraf's bedroom door after I was done with everything.

"Morning Amit..."

"Good morning. Still sleeping Saraf?"

"It's only nine. How come you got ready so early? Planning on going somewhere?"

"Nah... I just wanted to discuss about last night's dream."

"Okay. By the way, I'm out of smokes. Do you have any?"

"Yes, let me get the packet from my room."

I lit two and gave one to Saraf.

"Ah..." Saraf blows out a few rings after along drag. "The first smoke of the day has a very different taste."

"Yes, it's the most pleasurable of the day."

"Okay, tell me."

I told him the dream from beginning to end.

"Hmm... That was really strange. You have really developed some solid willpower within you."

"That means?"

"That pilot ran to you and promised to save you, right?"

"Yeah..."

"What exactly was he saying?"

"'Nothing will happen to you...'; 'I will save you...'"

"And what you were thinking about just before going to sleep?"

"Oh my, the same thing…"

"Exactly… Which means it was your mind that sent the pilot to send the message. That was your mind that successfully put yourself at the airport."

"Yes… That means I can go anywhere in my dreams."

"Yes. But that depends on your unconscious mind. If you can control that while sleeping, then you can travel anywhere and can even do anything in the dream at your whim. And you have already controlled your unconscious mind to some extent."

"So what should I do now?"

"I don't know how far this is practically possible. But you could be the most powerful person in your dreams and nothing can harm you in there as the story will be created by you yourself."

"That means I can direct my dream just like a film and I can give any role to anybody."

"Yes. And the best part is you won't even know that you are in a dream now and can feel the liveliness of the dream just you are feeling reality."

"Oh, Yes. This will be great… Hey, how about we go one step further?"

"What more is left after all this?"

"Is it possible the life I'm living now may be a dream itself? And only I can feel it and everyone else is here just to fill up my dream?"

"*(Laughs)* don't get cocky! I know I'm alive now and I can feel myself."

"May be you're just saying that because I wanted you to say it?"

"Oh, yeah...? Then why aren't you a pop star like Sahir Khan here? Why just an engineer? Heck, it might be my dream and you are just filler person inside mine?!"

"*(Laughs)* it's so complicated man!"

"Yes, the human mind is the most complicated thing because it can think of anything with its imagination."

My mobile rang- Unknown number...

"Hello"

"Hello, am I speaking to Amit Khanna?" A lady asked from the other side.

"Yes, Amit here"

"Sir, I'm Reeta calling from *Air Speed* broadband service."

"Finally, I get to hear from you people."

"Sir, you have not paid the billing amount of last month yet. Your billing due date was 2nd August."

"No, My billing due date was 5th august and I already paid the said amount. May be you are calling to wrong person."

"No sir, your billing due date was changed and we had sent a mail--"

"Whatever, I already paid the bill."

"No sir, I just checked the register and it is still not paid. Kindly clear pending payment by today's evening otherwise we might have to disconnect the services."

"How do you people get away with doing this to your customers? I told you the payments are clear."

"But sir—"

"I won't pay a single pie. Do whatever you want. I'm hanging up and will register a complaint immediately."

"Wait... Wait!" She started laughing loudly.

"Hello? Is this supposed to be funny?"

"You really didn't recognize my voice Amit?"

"Idiot...! You spoke to me in an altered voice! Whose number is this anyway?"

"It's me. Anushka." My face started glowing. "Guess what?"

"What?" I played it cool.

"I'm in Bangalore now. This is my new number."

"Great...! What brings you here all of a sudden?"

"I got a job here. For the moment I'm staying in a temporary guest house provided by company."

"Nice! You do realize you owe us a treat now for this, right?"

"That's why I called you. Shall we go for lunch today?"

"Sure, why not!"

"Saraf also stays with you, isn't it?"

"Yes, he is here."

"Good! Invite him as well."

"Sure, but where?"

"Why don't you recommend a good restaurant? I'm new to this city."

"Okay. Where are you right now?"

"M.G. Road."

"All right, can you head to Indiranagar? It will be 4 to 5 kilometres from M.G. Road."

"Sure. What's the name of the place?"

"There is a nice restaurant called "Taste of Nation". I'll text you the details."

"Cool. Then we'll be meeting at one o'clock?"

"Done... See you."

I was so happy. I texted the address. I was so excited!

"Hey, let's get ready." I said getting up.

"Why?" Saraf asked.

"Anushka got a job here in Bangalore and invited us for a treat."

"Oh... That's why you look so happy now!"

"Yes, of course. She is the only girl in my life I cared about. And at last God has listened to my prayers by bringing her near to me."

"I See. So, now that she is in Bangalore your love story might finally get some pace. Don't wait for anything. Propose to her today itself."

"What? No! Not today my friend. I have to wait for the right time to express my feelings."

"Today is the right time. Both of you will be alone. Just tell her man."

"Why? You're not coming?"

"Nope. I will catch up with her some other day. Today you go and have some confidence in yourself."

"I'm not sure how she will react. We are good friends. What do you think?"

"As far as I can tell, she likes you too."

"How the hell do you know that?"

"Just guessing... I have seen her attitude towards you. Girls seldom put the first steps towards a relationship. You have to land the first step. And girls love a courageous and confident guy who dares to admit how he feels towards her."

"All right, so how do I start?"

"Be original. Don't throw any filmy dialogue to express your love. Just go and talk to her straight from your heart. And don't sever eye contact when you talk."

"But what if she doesn't reciprocate?"

"There is a very rare chance of that happening. But even if she does, she won't hurt you directly. She might reply in a polite and diplomatic manner. Or maybe she'll tell you that she'll think about it. Anyway, it'll be good for you. At least you'll fulfil your duty of expressing your emotions. That itself will be a huge weight of your chest. The rest you'll have to leave on your luck."

"Hmm... I'll get ready then."

"Whatever you do please be honest with her. Do NOT follow a movie script!"

"Yeah... Yeah..."

I left the room and went for a bath. Saraf's words gave me little confidence. But I was still feeling very nervous.

"Amit today is an important day for you. You have to say it what's on your mind. Even if it doesn't go as you want it to, you can at least move on with your life without hoping for anything with her, right? Now go. Do it."

I reached the restaurant by quarter to one. I stood by the gate patiently looking around for Anushka. An auto grinds to a halt nearby and I saw Anushka step out. My belly was churning out of both anxiety and elation. I gave a subtle smile as she walked towards me and she smiled back.

"Hey, Amit...! So nice to see you after such a long time!" She exclaimed as she reached out for a hug.

"Me too...!" I said behind her ear as we hugged.

"Where is Saraf?"

For a moment there I panicked, Saraf and I never went over this part. "Oh, he had an important meeting come up. He had to attend."

"But it's a weekend..."

"For software engineers, there are no weekends! We have to work whenever it's necessary. You joined recently, right? You'll get a taste of the situation in no time."

"Maybe... But I'm still very excited to work in this industry."

"Yes we too remember the same excitement when we joined... But you get over it after a year. Anyway, let's go inside."

"Wait!"

She dialled someone up from her mobile.

"(On the phone) hello, how far are you? (Gap) okay, we are going inside then. Get here soon!"

"Is anyone else joining us?"

"Yes, it's a surprise! Now let's get inside. I have so many things to tell you."

We went inside. The maître de escorted us to the table I had already reserved.

"This is one of my favourite restaurants in Bangalore. The best part here is the starter menu. It is so good that sometimes I don't even bother with the main course."

"Really...? What's the specialty here?"

"Tandoori grills and seekh kebabs mostly... They serve all types of tikkas and kebabs. Look here, an electric fire under the table. And here are different types of sauces and seasonings. You need to baste the sauce on the kebabs or whatever and grill them to your liking before you eat."

"Yum... That sounds good!"

"Shall we order then?"

"Oh, Wait..."

She reached for her mobile. "Where are you? It's quarter past one already. Oh, get inside the restaurant then, we are sitting at the corner table on the left. Yes, yes, I can see you." A dashing guy in black shades walked towards us. He was tall, may be around 6 feet, light in complexion with a goatee. He hugged her and planted a small kiss on her cheek.

"Meet Amit, he was a senior in my college and also became one of my best friends." Anushka introduced me with such enthusiasm.

"Hi..." He said shaking my hand.

"This is Sayak. My love and my fiancé... surprise!" Anushka said.

I was speechless and in shock. My heart totally sank. Both of them were smiling and gazing at my face. I felt like running out from that place.

"Amit, What are you doing? Control your expressions! Put a damn smile on your face! Don't let them know the state you're in." I thought to myself as I tried to act like I was happy.

"Oh! Big surprise Anushka! Uh… Yes! Congratulations…!"

"Thank you Amit!"

"Uh Sayak… Please do sit down. I'll place the order."

"Excuse me waiter, we are ready." I shouted.

"Vegetarian or non-vegetarian" waiter stood there with his notepad.

"Anushka, you are non-veg right? And Sayak…?"

"He is too."

"Okay, two non-veg and one veg please."

"So you are vegetarian?" Sayak asked.

"No, no, only on Thursdays and Saturdays he abstains from non-vegetarian. Isn't that right Amit?"

"Yup…"

I couldn't pretend everything was fine and keep speaking anymore. A lot of noise ran through my mind… I didn't want to sit there. So I took out my mobile phone and faked a phone call.

"Excuse me; I'll be back in two minutes. I need to get this. You please carry on."

I left the table and walked out of the restaurant as fast as I could. My eyes began to water and I started laughing at the same time. In spite of being in public I couldn't resist the urge to talk to myself again.

"Amit, you are such a fool. You think you are a hero? You are a hero in your dreams only. Look at her and look at you. She is an angel. How the heck did you ever expect her to fall in love with you?!"

"But I thought that deep inside she had always had feelings for me. I guess all girls are the same. They don't need love. They need looks and money."

"Just shut up, will you? Don't talk like that about Anushka. It's you who's the loser which is why you are bad mouthing other people."

"What should I tell her then? You know how much I love her."

"But did you see her say anything of that sort? Pray to God that Sayak has the fortitude to be a nice partner for her... Now get back inside, it's extremely rude to leave them behind like this. And stop with that pathetic look on your face, wallowing in sorrow. Go inside and put on a happy look"

I went back feigning an exaggerated smile.

"Sorry to make you wait so long."

"No problem."

"When did you become so formal Amit?!"

"Not towards you Anushka. I was just trying to impress Sayak." Everybody laughed and I pretended away.

We finished the lunch and went outside.

"See you Amit, I'll call you later."

"Sure. Bye. Take care."

I tried so hard not to cry but my mind couldn't hold back my tears. I felt like a beggar on the street who had lost everything in life. I just kept walking down the road. There was nothing left in this world for me. I went to an empty parking lot and started chain smoking.

"It's okay Amit. Forget about her..." I started talking to myself again "You have a full career and life ahead of you. You'll find a better girl than Anushka."

"May be but I'll never get Anushka."

"So what...? Don't forget there's a lot more that this world has to offer to enjoy. Let's party today. Enjoy life... One day you'll die anyway... Call Saraf."

I dialled Saraf. My watery eyes made it hard to focus on the screen.

"Hello Saraf?"

"Yeah...? Why so late buddy? Both of you're going for dinner as well?! (Laughs)"

"Nah... Nothing of the sort... I'll tell you everything. Please come to Domlur. I'm standing near the fly over near Taste of Nation."

"Why? What happened? Your voice doesn't sound normal. Is there anything wrong?"

"I'll tell you later. Please come soon. By the way, don't take your bike take an auto."

"Huh? Why?"

"No more questions. Just come here."

Saraf shows up half an hour later. He notices the sadness on my face.

"What happened dude? Where is Anushka?"

I couldn't stop my eyes. The tears just didn't stop. I was crying like a child. Saraf understood everything.

"Oh, come on now. Everything will be fine."

"I loved her from the core of my heart... Why do people fall in love Saraf? Does God enjoy seeing people in pain?"

"I'm not sure man. Maybe if everybody had a good time all the time, they wouldn't appreciate the value of happiness. Just like if there was no summer we wouldn't appreciate the monsoon. Life is about experiencing everything... The good and the bad... Let's go to a bar and just relax."

"Yes, that's why I told you not to take the bike."

We then went to the nearest bar and stayed up late. I drank a little too much and was in and out of consciousness.

"That's enough now. Let's go home."

"Sa—rafff... (Hic) why did she do this to me? Why did she (hic) always give me that smile of a lover? I'm free now... (Hic) I can do whatever I want. I'll stay here."

"Please, I'm your friend, right? Then why you are giving more importance to people who are not here with you? I'm here with you right now. Let's go. "

Saraf put my arms around his shoulders and helped me outside.

"You stand here. Let me get an auto."

"Hi Doggy... (Hic)" I started talking to a street dog. "You seem so happy today. Thank God (hic) that you are not a person. You can fuck anyone you want. May be I'll also be a dog. Please be my (hic) friend doggy. Come shake my hand."

"Stop behaving like that. Let's go."

"Saraf, you know a dog (hic) is the most trusted animal in the world?"

"Yes..."

"And God is totally the opposite. That's why if you (hic) spelt "dog" backwards you will get "god". (Laughs)"

"Just shut up. Don't think like that. Time will heal your pain... It always does."

"Why? Are you afraid that if God hears this he will punish you as well?"

"Just get in the auto; you are totally out of your senses right now."

He pushed me into the auto. I rested my head against the tarpaulin sides and fell asleep."

Dream Log:

I was in a dance bar. I was dancing like a joker there. Just then I heard someone calling me.

"Amit... Amit!"

I woke up.

"Hey, we're home. Step out of the auto."

"Oh, I was in a dream again Saraf. I was dancing. It was a short dream but a nice dance. May be I'll dance now too." I started dancing the same way I was dancing in the dream.

"Uh oh, how do I control you now? Get in your room."

I felt like throwing up. I went to the toilet and started puking. Saraf was holding my head up. I was feeling so weak.

"It's ok... vomiting is good. It's your body's way of getting rid of the alcohol in your stomach. Go get some sleep now."

He took me to the bed and made sure I lay on my side. That way I won't choke on my own vomit in case I puke in my sleep. Just as he switched off the lights I felt I was going to black out. I started talking to myself again.

"Anushka, you are mine... I love you so much. I can't live without you. You are mine Anushka. You are mine." murmuring I went into a deep sleep.

Dream Log:

I found myself walking on a huge desert. There was nothing except a big ocean of sand. I didn't know where I was going... just kept walking. I was so thirsty and I started shouting "water... water..."

Sometime later I saw what appeared to be a big tent over the horizon. I started walking towards it but I couldn't reach it. It seemed to be moving away the more I moved towards it. Night fell all of a sudden and I saw lots of colourful lights emitting from the tent. I was still so thirsty and kept shouting for water.

Finally I made it there. It was a big decorated house. I went inside and found people everywhere. Everybody just stood there with plates of roasted tikka in their hands. I was so thirsty and looked all over for water. I screamed into peoples' faces "someone please give me some water!" But no one listened. Everybody was busy talking with each other. There was a food stall near the gate. I went there.

"Please, some water..."

One of the waiters gave me a plate and served some chicken on it. I burst out with uncontrollable anger. I threw the plate and again shouted for water. There was no response from anybody. It felt as if I was shouting in French and nobody really understood.

I tried to ask every soul there for water. I went over to all the people in the party, one by one. Shook their hands and asked for water. But no one replied, just stared at me.

So much food everywhere... but not a drop of water anywhere... I prayed to God for some water.

I put my hands inside my pocket and found a lot of money. I showed the bundle of notes to everybody - "Please take all money. But give me a glass of water please!"

No response. I started running here and there till I found another gate. I went through that and another group of people are just standing and looking in one direction. I couldn't make out what they are looking. I forced myself through the crowd and saw a big "mandap" erected there. Anushka and Sayak sat together and a pundit was chanting mantras. Anushka looked so beautiful in her bridal attire. I couldn't understand what was going on. Was she getting married?

"Stop this marriage! I'm Anushka's only true love. Anushka is mine."

But nobody cared. Everyone just ignored me. I felt no one could hear my voice. I was like an inanimate object there. I tried to run towards the "mandap" but someone held onto me from behind. I was still shouting - "Anushka, I love you so much. Please don't marry anybody else. I will give you everything you ever wanted in life. I'll never let you feel lonely. I will love you like you're my God Anushka. Please get out from there. Please Anushka! Please... I can't live without you. You are mine. You are mine... Oh, God please help me! Please help... me..." I was crying so loudly.

"Yanna Rascala, Mind It! This marriage won't happen." The pundit suddenly stood up and put on some black goggles – à la Rajnikanth – and exclaimed.

"Sayak, I never expected this from you." Anushka also stood up and gave Sayak a tight slap. "Trying to marry me forcefully... You imbecile! Get out of here; I love Amit. Amit I'm coming!"

Someone pulled my arm from behind.

"Here is your water sir." It was the same waiter from the banquet but with a glass of water this time.

I felt so happy to see a glass of water. Within a couple of seconds I chugged it all down and threw the empty glass up in joy.

I turned around and saw Anushka running towards me. Without a word she held me tightly and planted kisses all over my face. From somewhere I heard a song playing in the air –

"Tere ghar aya, Mein aya tujhko lene...

Dil ke badle me, dil ka nazrana dene!

Mere har dhadkan kya bole hai, sun... sun... sun..."

Everybody there started dancing and singing in chorus "Sajan ji ghar aye."

Anushka was still in my arms. I was so happy at the time... I have never been this happy ever. The revelry with song and dance went on for a long time...

...Until, I got up. Oh, No. It was just a dream. How I wished for it to be real. First time ever I had such a sweet dream. I didn't want to wake up at all. I closed my eyes again and started remembering the dream in hopes of going back to sleep and back to the same dream. I tried to sleep but couldn't. I could only imagine the dream. But I was aware it was just my imagination but and I was not really dreaming. When I didn't want to dream it would inevitably come. But now that I want to dream I can't sleep. If only I could have such dreams every day, I wouldn't have anything to complain about.

I finally got up from bed and washed up. For some reason I wasn't feeling a hangover at all that morning. I went to Saraf's room. He was surfing the net.

"Good morning Saraf."

"Good morning. Are you feeling all right now?"

"Absolutely fresh...! Although, I'm extremely sorry about last night..."

"Don't worry about it. If I was in your situation, I would have done more."

"Thanks dude. Anyway, I had a really nice dream last night."

"Nice...?! After such a tragedy how did you possibly manage to have a nice dream? I was worried about you that you would be having some of the most horrible dreams ever."

"Yes, it started horribly but it became sweeter and sweeter. And the ending was so good that I want to have this dream every night."

I recanted the whole dream to Saraf.

"So strange Amit; you are really developing a strong mind inside that brain of yours. You have come so far. I have never seen anyone with such tremendous willpower. You have already started playing with your dreams."

"Yes Saraf. I was so thirsty and I was shouting for water. But nobody was listening to me. I was crying like anything when I saw Anushka was getting married."

"Yes, that was supposedly the crucial part of the dream.   . But your mind has changed the way you dream so drastically. It's changed the game now. I mean you used to have all those dreams against your wishes whereas now your mind is showing you the things, that your heart really wishes to see."

"Yes, that's true. But I still can't believe Anushka is not mine in reality."

"Please don't remind yourself of those things now. You should feel good that you won't have bad dreams anymore, right?"

"Yeah, I guess. Now I only want to live in my dreams. You know there were some instances that were so funny in that dream. Like the pundit putting on the black shades and talking like Rajnikanth. And also all the filmy dancing and singing!"

"Yes, that was funny. But funny is good; those were good things in your dream."

Saraf and I continued discussing the dream at length.

Ever since that day I never had any bad dream. My dreams became sweeter with each passing night. My waking life became so much better from that day on. But I still missed Anushka sometimes. I always tried to avoid her calls and ignored her texts and emails. Month's go by and I eventually stopped getting any correspondence from her side.

October 1ˢᵗ, 2011.

It was Saturday and I had a pretty good dream last night. I woke up and felt so refreshed. I lay on bed thinking - now that I have enough power to make my dreams better, could I just set my dreams to any time I wanted? What if I started dreaming and set myself in any situation and any place? Would it be possible to put myself anywhere I wanted when I start dreaming? That would be great. I must try this.

That night I was watching a Hollywood movie and I saw a nice beach. I had always wanted to travel the world. I'll do it someday. I would go to Australia first and stay there for a week just on in this beach only. It was so beautiful and the people were either surfing, water skiing or riding on jet bikes. I wish I could do this.

Saraf walked in.

"What's the movie you are watching?" Saraf asked.

"Hey, come. Look at that beach. Isn't it so beautiful?" I rested my chin on my palm.

"Yes, it looks nice. Do you know how to water ski?"

"How do I do this? I want to do this so bad."

"Last year, when I went to Goa for that conference, I got a chance to water ski."

"Oh, really...? What was it like?"

"At first I was so nervous because I didn't know how to swim. But they provided a life jacket and assured me there were life guards all around so I went ahead with it. I really enjoyed it."

"Then let's plan a trip to Goa someday."

"Sure. I have another conference there in February. You can tag along. It's very nice place."

"Okay, then done. We are going to Goa in February."

"All right, carry on with your fantasizing. (Laughs) I need to go to sleep now; I have to get up early tomorrow morning for some work."

"Okay, Good Night."

I went to bed around 11 after the movie ended. I thought about dreaming of the beach I saw in the movie. I realized that I should start experimenting with that idea right away - of trying to put myself anywhere on the earth. But how...? May be I should watch the beach scene again and again.

I copied the movie to my mobile and went to the bed. I had the latest smartphone at that time which could render 2D clips to 3D. Not full 3D of course but it showed a simulated pseudo-3D view pretty well. I switched off the lights and started watching those beach scenes over and over again. Then I tried to imagine myself on that beach. I closed my eyes and put myself there. I was imagining myself water skiing. I could see that my face blurred out in my imagination. An hour later I had fallen asleep completely.

Dream Log:

I was in a big jungle. I crept ahead with a machete in my hand. With that I was hacking the thicket out of my way. Suddenly the forest scenery was vanishing in and out of existence replaced by the view of the ocean. It was just like changing an analogue TV channel frequently between two channels. Then the flickering stopped and again I could see myself in the jungle. A few steps ahead I saw a clear blue sky straight through the forest canopy. As I moved forward I heard the sound of waves crashing on the shore; the trees and the undergrowth cleared away and I found myself at the edge of a cliff. From there I could see miles of ocean in front of me. I peered down and saw the water crashing against the rocks. I looked at the distance and saw a beach which was far away from this place.

"Now how do I reach the beach? I wish I had a big ship." As soon as I finished the thought I heard the loud horn of an ocean liner. It was harboured a mile off shore. "Shall I swim to it now? No, no. It's too far. I don't have the stamina and also I'm feeling so tired right now." I started shouting- "Can anyone send a shore boat for me?" Just like that, I saw a small boat heading towards me. Within a few minutes it reached the rocks at the bottom of the cliff. I dived into the water like they do in Acapulco and climbed into the boat. I found a young maiden operating the motor on the boat.

"Hi, I'm Amit." I said shaking her left hand as she steered the rudder with the other.

"I'm Annie."

"Thanks for getting me out of here Annie."

"It was my pleasure sir."

"Just call me Amit."

"Okay, Amit. Where do you want to go now? The beach or the liner...?"

"How about the beach...?"

"Sure. Anything else you want?"

"Do you have some chilled beer?"

"Of course. Here you go."

She handed me a chilled beer from a wine-cooler. I enjoyed the wind in my hair while sipping my beer as we made our way to the beach.

We made shore in a few minutes. It was such a big beautiful beach. People everywhere; some played volleyball, some just swam. Few lay there on lawn chairs with an umbrella on top.

I went running to a guy that seemed like a lifeguard. I went to him and asked for a swim suit. He pointed me to a small cottage where I found lots of nice swimming costumes. I put on one and went back.

I felt so alone though. If only I could have had some friends around. That would have been great.

"Excuse me." I turned and standing there were three sexy girls with their toned arms around each other's shoulder.

"Yes?"

"Would you mind playing volleyball with us? There are three of us, we need one more." one of them said.

"Sure. Let's go."

We played for a while. Later I tried all types of water sports there. I was really enjoying the place. It seemed so alien compared to our busy everyday world. No stress, no work. Just peace and leisure...

At sunset, one of the lifeguards asked me to get ready. He took me to a very nice hotel near the beach. I took a hot shower and put on a designer Hawaiian shirt and khaki pant. I went back to the beach and found a banquet table with candles of all sizes and shapes set on it. People were eating and drinking by the candle light. I found those three girls waiting for me. They invited me over to their side.

What an experience! A long table with candles, chairs set such that you could feel the water touching your feet, delicious fried shrimp and an open bar. I spent the evening away talking with girls. We even started flirting with each other. I felt like a VIP there! Thus the night went on.

Then I woke up. Goddammit! It was only a dream! I wished I could have stayed there forever. I sat up on my bed and tried to remember the whole dream. I started writing all of it down for my thesis - the part about how one could create situations inside dreams. This was a significant moment. Before, I was only able to bring about changes that would have saved me from dangerous situations. But now I could put myself in any situation I desired. I thought I should discuss this with Saraf.

(Knock on door).

"Hey Amit... Why are up so early today?"

"Dude, I can't wait to share something amazing news with you."

"What the good news?"

"I can go anywhere in my dreams. I can fully control them now."

"Really...?! What did you dream last night?"

I told him about how I went over the clips on my mobile before going to sleep and how I then started using my imagination before all that happened in my dreams.

"This is a miracle Amit. How would you say, you felt in your dream?"

"It felt real Saraf. I was myself just like I'm in real life. I could even taste the shrimp as if it was real."

"That means you can have everything you ever wanted in those seven to eight hours of sleep."

"Yes, I can become a famous star like Shahrukh Khan or be the prime minister of India. Heck, I could be President of the U.S.! A famous scientist? Or a rich investor! The best part is I'll feel as if it's real."

"That's great!"

"Yeah, but the caveat is that I'll wake up and find it was all in my dreams."

"So what...? At least you'll know that eighteen hours later you'll be in paradise again!"

"Yes. I'll pretend these boring waking hours of my day as a dream and will live a nice life back in my dreams."

Henceforth, I started dreaming just as I wanted. Sometime I would be a famous movie star then on other occasions a famous cricketer. Anything in this world that I couldn't be or get, I would in my dreams. I started fulfilling some of my fantasies. I had girlfriends all over the world, each more beautiful than the next. Wherever I would see a sexy girl in real life, whether at the office or on the street, I would manifest them in my dream and had my way. I got everything in life I could have ever wanted. Later on I thought I should sleep a little more so that I could enjoy my dream life for longer. So I started taking sleeping pills to sleep longer. Sometimes I even took them just after waking up to go back in again. I didn't have any interest in my work. My work performance dropped off. I started getting warnings from my manager. I wasn't happy with my real life.

By 2016 Saraf had married and I was staying alone in the flat. One day I decided to quit my job. But for that I needed a small amount of constant cash flow to survive. I started writing blogs and developed a couple of websites. I put ads on them and traffic along with revenue increased day by day.

In 2018 I resigned. I planned to move away from this busy city and lead the rest of my life somewhere peacefully. When I left the company, I got a lump sum of money as gratuity and superannuation. I also encased my fixed deposits. I got around eighty-five lakh rupees in total. I moved to the outskirts of Mumbai and built a small cottage. I started living there away from the crowds.

February 2ⁿᵈ, 2019.

The cricket world cup started. I loved watching cricket. It was the only thing from reality that I cared to pay attention to. India played England for the first game of the world cup. I didn't take any sleeping pills that day and watched the match. Unfortunately, India lost by 6 runs. I was so disappointed. I stayed up thinking about the match – It was the first match of the world cup and India lost. Why were they playing like that? If India had won I could have gone to sleep tonight really happy after a long time. Then I said to myself "Forget about the real world cup. Why can't I play world cup in my dream and India will win all the matches and take the trophy!" At least in my dreams I would have felt it was as real and be proud and happy that India won. My mind was made. I have been dreaming about being stars or politicians. Now, for few days I would be dreaming the world cup. I chose to be a batsman to start thing off.

I closed my eyes and imagined a cricket stadium filled to the brim. As an opening batsman I was imagining myself hitting furs and sixes on every ball. Eventually I had fallen asleep and started playing in my dream. In it I was a famous batsman and hitting ball like anything. India won its first match against England that day.

After that I stopped watching cricket in my real life. The only interesting phenomenon from real life that I could enjoy was abandoned too. I didn't get a taste of my real life at all apart from the bills, errands and sundries. India started wining every match and took the trophy in the world cup. Of course, that's in my dreams only. I didn't have any knowledge about what transpired in the world cup in reality. I didn't want to know it. For me India had won, even if it was just in my dreams.

May 22nd, 2019.

I woke up from a nice dream. I finished taking notes for my thesis and went for a bath. I decided to go to the market to buy some vegetables. There was a very small market near my cottage. I lived in a small village actually and it was a temporary market where people sat on the road side and sold all types of vegetables and fruits. But that day I didn't find any vendor. I went to a small tea stall near the place.

"Half a cup and one *Gold Flake*." I told the boy sitting behind the stove stirring the kettle.

I drew a long puff of the cigarette and thought to myself "What do I do now? There's no food left at home."

"Do you know where all the vendors on the road side are?" I asked the boy.

"I don't know sab. They have not been here for two days."

"Oh. Is there any other market here where I can buy something? Or, any restaurants nearby...?"

"Not here. But there are many *'dhabas'* by the highway."

"How far it is? Is it at walking distance?"

"That I don't know. I tend to the tea stall and live here only. But you can get a bus from there" he replied by pointing towards the highway bus stop.

"Ok, Thanks" I finished my tea and moved out.

I reasoned that if I had to travel by bus I might as well just go to city. Then I can buy some fresh vegetables from the supermarket. I reached the highway and boarded a bus. After I got down I straightaway went to the nearest supermarket there.

I didn't want to spend any time back in the city more than I had to. I got some vegetables and eggs in the cart and pushed it towards the counter. Suddenly, I heard someone calling me from behind.

"Hey, Amit... Amit...!"

I turned around and froze. I was totally surprised. Not the good kind either. It was Anushka. Time slowed down and for a moment there I started talking to myself - "Oh, God Why? Why can't you let her leave me alone? What did I ever do to you?"

She rushed towards me in the meantime and stared at me with surprised looks.

"I can't believe it's you! Where have you been all these years? You totally dropped off the map! And what's with the long hair, full beard? Have you become a sadhu or some baba or what?"

"Uh... Hey, Anushka! What are you doing in Mumbai?"

"That's a long story. What about you Amit? Why are donning such a look?!"

"Not because of the reasons you cited. I just prefer to keep a full beard and flowing locks that's all." I feigned a chuckle.

"I tried to reach you many times. But your phone was always switched off and then eventually went out of service. Even Saraf doesn't have your address or your new number. Please tell me if you still consider me as one of your best friends" She asked sternly.

"It's nothing like that Anushka. Honest. But seriously though, tell me about you. How is life treating you?"

"Amit, I know you are hiding something from me. Anyway, don't share." She stood there folding her hands and turning away.

"Hey, don't get angry. Actually, I have become weary of this busy world. So I decided to undertake a spiritual sojourn and rest somewhere peacefully. That's why you see me with the long hair and the beard."

"But why Amit...? Why this suddenly? You had a good career going. Why are you throwing all of this away? I honestly feel bad seeing you like this." "Don't feel bad. Really, I'm happy now. I'm enjoying my life more than I ever did. Anyway forget all that. Tell me about you. When did you move to Mumbai?"

"Huh? Why are you even asking? You don't seem to care about anyone anymore. You stopped all contact with me. I tried so many times but you didn't pick up my calls." She said coyly.

"I'm extremely sorry about that. Things happened really fast. I don't have contact with any of my friends. Not even Saraf."

"You are really changed Amit. Anyway, my husband got a transfer here in Mumbai. So I had to quit my job and we settled down here"

"Oh... So, how is Sayak--"

"What?? Sayak...?"She interrupted with crazy looks.

"Yeah, you just said you settled down here with your husband..."

"Oh god, you don't know anything then, do you?"

"Why? What happened?" I was taken aback. "The day we got together you said he was your fiancé. ...Sayak, right?"

"Right, he was Sayak. But we never got married. We broke up after a month..."

"What...!" I asked with a tensed tone.

"Yes. He cheated on me. We had a serious fight and broke it off"

"But-- But-- God... Why didn't you tell me?"

"I tried reaching you many times. But you were not picking up my calls. I was so upset at the time. Nobody was there with me. I went through such a bad phase. Anyway, I managed to get over it."

I was feeling so much regret then that I got angry at myself but somehow I controlled it.

"Then who did you marry after all?" I asked.

"Well, after four years my parents arranged my marriage. I went ahead without a word. I thought at least my parents' choice would be better than mine. And it was. He is a nice man and I'm happy."

I was speechless. I was crying and beating myself up in my head.

"Anyway, let's get some coffee somewhere." She asked me.

I did not reply. I was so zoned out.

"Hello, Amit?"

"Oh, Yes, yes."

"What are you thinking?"

"Nothing... Yes tell me..."

"I asked can we get some coffee."

"Well, Sorry." I took my time and said. "I have some urgent work right now. We will catch up some other day."

"Okay, give me your number."

"Well, I don't have a mobile. Now that I am a hermit, I don't like to carry that burden anymore. You give me yours, I'll call you."

"Are you sure? Or will you disappear again?"

"No. I'll definitely call you."

I was screaming at myself after I got home. "You idiot...! What have you done? If only you had picked up the calls then Anushka could have been yours. You ruined your own life" My eyes started to water. "God...? What game are you playing with me? I was living alone so happily here, Why did you bring Anushka back into my life and let me know the truth about her and Sayak? My love for her led me to sacrifice everything." I cried aloud.

I couldn't eat anything that day. I was living in the past thinking about Anushka after ages. I lay on my bed thinking about what could have been all night. I started fighting with myself.

"Stop it Amit. Stop thinking about Anushka please!"

"What do I do Amit? She is coming back again and again. What a big mistake..."

"I'm really sorry. You were so upset back then; I thought I took the best course of action. If only you had talked to her, I wouldn't have repressed my feelings for her in spite of knowing about her fiancé. Please think of something else instead of thinking about her before you fall asleep. Otherwise she will haunt your dream."

"Okay. I'll try to think about some superstar. Yes, I will be Shahrukh Khan tonight."

I kept imagining myself him after I closed my eyes and as always after few minutes I went into a deep sleep.

Dream Log:

It was a nice morning. I had just awakened. I went outside to a big garden in my front yard. There was an electric cart parked near the house. I climbed in and drove around the garden. It was huge and after a few minutes I saw a big umbrella covering some chairs and a table. I stopped and got out to be greeted by a guy in white.

"Good morning sir. Your tea is ready. "He said with a big smile.

"Thank you Johnny, Where is Teena?"

"She will be here soon, sir. Anything else...?"

"No. You may go."

"Okay Sir." he left.

I started reading the newspaper that was kept on the table. The warm sunshine made some parts of the garden shimmer golden. A gentle breeze blew. Minutes later Teena, my secretary, showed up. Gorgeous with green eyes...

"Good morning Amit. Did you sleep well?"

"Good morning! Yes it was good. So what's the schedule for today?"

"At ten you have a shooting at R K Studios. Then at four you have a meeting with Rohit Shetty for his next movie 'Singham Forever'. At six you have an interview with Stars magazine. Then at night you have flight for Rome. The entire crew will be there and shooting will start as soon as you get there."

"Oh, yes. I forgot about that. How many days there? Seven right?"

"Yes. I have already made the arrangements for you. Both your personal doctor and trainer are there already and will be with you the whole time."

"Thanks Teena. I wonder how I could've managed all this if you weren't with me. Anyway I'll be ready for my shower in twenty minutes. You carry on."

"Ok Amit" She left.

I swiped to unlock my iPad and opened my twitter.

"Good morning guys! I'll be flying to Rome for the final phase of shooting for 'Dhoom 5'"

I tweeted. I looked at the top of the screen and sent another.

"Wow, surpassed 1 billion followers today! I must start doing Hollywood movies now as well. Thanks, to all my fans!"

After surfing the web some more I got up and instantly reached R K Studios. .

I was on a wide road with lots of fans on either side. The security guards held the ropes tight so that nobody would rush onto me. "Amit...! Amit...!" They shouted. There were signs everywhere. One of the girls carried one on that said, "I won't lose my virginity without Amit!"

I was so excited. The director came over.

"You need to drive the bike from here to there. Your speed should be twenty kilometres per hour. Do NOT exceed that. Remember, only twenty. We will speed it up by adjusting camera speed. At that point you remove your helmet and throw it on the road. The police jeep will ride over your helmet and it'll start to rattle and swerve. Eventually it'll lose balance, start rolling on the road and fly over your bike and then land in a huge explosion. Your stunt man is ready. He'll take your place just after you throw the helmet"

"Stunt man...?! You know I do my own stunts, right?. I can do it myself."

"Are you sure? This shot is really risky. The police jeep will be few inches above the bike."

"Not a problem. You just start shooting."

Then the director moved away from the road and said "Action" from behind the camera monitor. I started the bike and drove it till 20 KMph. It was a very long road. A police jeep started following me having with a loud siren. After crossing a flag I removed the helmet and threw my helmet at the front tire of the jeep. The skilled driver made the jeep rattle and swerve. When they pulled the rope tied to the jeep it started rolling. Just as it went over my head I saw a familiar face sitting beside the driver. It seemed time slowed down for a few moments. Everything moved slower. The jeep was there over my head and it was moving frame by frame. I could clearly her shout "Amit Help! Help me Amit!"

I went over thoughts in fractions of a second. "Who is this girl? I think I have seen her somewhere before. How did she know my name? May be she's one of my fans. But how she is in the jeep? I should save her. But it is too risky. Aha! I can be superhero. "I then jumped through the jeep's windshield breaking in. I was rolling along with the jeep and holding the girl in my arms. After a few more rolls the jeep stopped. I saw that it was Anushka. I was hurt bad. I couldn't get myself up. I was going in and out of consciousness. Blood in my eyes made everything red. People rushed towards the jeep and pulled me out while I was still holding Anushka.

Suddenly, I found myself in a hospital. I'm lying on a gurney. I saw Teena standing beside me. I did not remember when I had closed my eyes but now they were fully open. The red tint from the blood was there no more.

"How do you feel Amit?" Teena asked.

"Umm... Better. How's the girl?"

"Which girl Amit...?"

"The girl in the jeep... I jumped into the jeep to save her."

"I think you had severe brain trauma. There was no girl inside the jeep. And you are here because the jeep hit you when it was supposed to jump over you."

"What? How it is that possible? I really saved a girl. I can remember her face so well."

"I think you had a bad dream and a bad concussion on top of that. It is all in your head. You take rest now. I have already cancelled all your meetings." She tried to reassure me.

"Dream...?! You think that was a dream? No! I know she was Anushka." I shouted.

"This is the dream. Yes Teena. I'm dreaming now."

"Doctor, Doctor..." Teena started to panic.

The doctor barged into the room with the nurses. They held my hands and legs down tightly.

"Leave me Doctor. This is a dream. I know that girl. She is Anushka. My love... My life..."

"You had a severe head injury Mr. Amit, that's why you are having these thoughts. We are all real. This is not a dream."

"Oh Yeah...? Let me prove you wrong." I started flying across the room. I started walking on the wall. I removed the roof from the hospital and started flying in the air.

"See, I'm flying now. Now, go ahead. Tell me this is not a dream."

Everybody below started laughing loudly...

...and I woke up from the dream.

Oh God. I started having scary dreams again. I lay in bed for an hour thinking about what had happened. I couldn't control my dream and I let Anushka come out from my memory again and forcefully entered my dream. I tried to convince myself that Anushka wasn't real. She just appeared as a dream but I was unsuccessful in my dream. How could I when I started flying like a bird in the sky? All my arguments stood defeated in front of myself when I declared it was a dream and started flying. The dream had become lucid.

It was eleven in the morning. I got up from bed and started writing down the dream in my diary. I was so hungry. I cooked some rice and egg curry. After finishing my lunch I went for a walk. I was still thinking about the dream. I went to a beach near my cottage and sat there for hours. I enjoyed the sunset on the beach. I came back to my cottage and ate the same rice and egg curry. I was so sad that day. I continued to think about Anushka. I wasn't feeling sleepy that night at all. I started drinking some wine. I finished a full bottle of wine and felt so uneasy. I lay down on my bed. Anushka's face flashed before my eyes over and over again. I tried to reason with myself.

"Amit, Please stop thinking about her. Please I'm requesting you. Otherwise there will be no meaning in living in my dreams anymore. She'll come again and again to ruin my sweet dreams" I said to myself.

"What do I do then? I can't stop thinking about her"

"Please Amit. You can do it. Forget that you met her again in Mumbai. Calm down and remind yourself about all the good dreams you used to have"

I took out a diary from the shelf and started reading a few of my beautiful dreams. After reading for a few hours I was sad again.

"In all my dreams I have everything - Money, power, travel, sex – all my desires and fantasies are fulfilled. But there is no 'love' in my dreams. Can't I dream that I'm just a normal person, not famous or rich? And have a cute girlfriend in my life who would love me dearly?"

"Yes, I should dream like that. Tonight I'll dream about real love and live a beautiful life."

"But what about the script...? Should I just imagine some random location with a beautiful girl?"

"No, that won't create emotions. You should make some logical script."

"But to create a logical story it will take days!"

"Okay, let's do one thing. Let's watch a romantic movie then you'll replace the male character with yourself."

"That sounds good. Which movie...?"

"Umm... what is a romantic movie that you like the most... Yes! *'Veer Zaara'*...!"

"No. Not *'Veer Zaara'*. There are too many tragedies in that movie. I don't want to stay in a jail for twenty two years. I should dream about something simpler. Something where the male character is not only in love with the girl, but also with everything else - the people, the natural beauty, the country. I mean I want to make myself feel real love. The sacred one..."

"*'Swades'*..."

"Hmm... Yes, *'Swades'* will be perfect. I'll have to create the same plot in my dream. Let me watch that movie again"

I downloaded *"Swades"* and started watching it again. It's a long movie. By the time I finished, it was two o'clock. It really is an evergreen movie. As many times as I had seen it, it gave me the same feelings I had when I watched it for the first time. I really loved that movie.

So, now I started imagining that I was the male character. I then took one sleeping pill and closed my eyes. I started thinking about the whole movie. I put myself in place of the Hero *"Mohan Bhargab"*. After a few minutes I started dreaming as usual.

Dream Log:

I was a NASA scientist and also the project manager of a project called "GPM". I was sitting with my colleagues at a press conference.

"What is the purpose of this project?" One journalist asked.

I was sitting in front of a mike so I started describing it-

"'GPM' refers to 'Global Precipitation Measurement'. We'll launch a satellite which will revolve around the earth and measure the amount of rainfall in various countries of the world. It will go through Australia, India, Africa--"

Before finishing the talk I stood up and started whispering "India... India. I need to go to India to meet Kaveri Amma.She is like my mother and loves me very much"

(Kaveri Amma was the household maid of the male character but she was also like a godmother to him when he was growing up.)

I then asked for permission from my boss who was sitting just beside me if I could go to India right now. "Don't you see you are talking in an *interview? What is wrong with you?"* He replied in anger. "Why are suddenly behaving like this?"

"I don't care anymore. I want to go to India right now. I want a month's leave." I became restless and screamed at him.

"Okay, Okay. Calm down. You can go. But delegate your responsibilities among your team members."

"Sure. I'll have a detailed team meeting with them." No sooner had I said this than I found myself on an airplane and then at an airport where one of my friends had come to receive me.

"How was the journey, Mohan?" My friend asked.

"To whom you are addressing?" I looked at either side of me with a surprised face. "I'm Amit man! How could you forget my name?" I asked him back.

"Oh, Sorry... Actually one of my friend's names is Mohan. So by mistake I called you Mohan."

(Actually Mohan was the lead male character's name in the movie. My unconscious mind forgot to change the character name to Amit here. But it controlled the situation and rectified it later)

"Did you get all information about Kaveri Amma or not?" I asked him.

"Yes, she stays in a village called Charanpur. It's about two hundred kilometres from here. You can take my car and meet her."

"No, no. I won't need a car. Actually I'm not sure how the facilities in such a small and remote village will be like. Can you arrange a caravan for me?"

Just as I said that I found myself driving the caravan. I was singing a song all the while too.

(The same song that was sung in the movie during the caravan scene.)

After sometime I reached Charanpur. I stopped the caravan just in front of a small "paan" shop. It was a very narrow road here.

"Excuse me; do you know where Kaveri Amma stays?" I asked the owner.

"Hey Chiku, take this gentleman to Kaveri Amma." He instructed a kid.

The kid then started running in front of my caravan and showed the way to Kaveri Amma's house. It was a very big house. I was standing outside when the kid went inside to call Kaveri Amma. I hid myself. When Kaveri Amma came out, I held my hands over her eyes from behind and asked her to identify me.

"Who is this? Leave me! Leave me!" She started screaming.

"Guess who I'm? Only then will I remove my hands."

"No. I can't guess. Please leave me!"

"Atkan batkan dahi chatokan, Tu yosodha, Mein hun--" I had started reciting a rhyme but she immediately stopped me. Her face started glowing with pleasure. She finished the rhyme by saying "Mohan... Mohan, I knew it! I knew that one day you'll come back to me."

"Mohan?" I was surprised again. "I'm Amit, Kaveri Amma."

"Yes... Yes, you are my Amit! I used to call you by Mohan when you're a child. Have you forgotten?"

"Oh Yes. It's been so long time that I forgot. You did use to call me Mohan."

(My mind again tricked me into thinking this was real and not a dream based on a movie. It created a temporary memory and convinced me that my other name is Mohan as well.)

As the time went on I gradually fell in love with the villagers, with nature, with my beautiful India and before long I fell in love with a girl. Everything went so smoothly and I was very happy.

One night I was sitting with Geeta. I held her hand and said, "Geeta, I'm really very happy here. I wasn't aware of such real pleasure when I was in America. I found everything there, all the comforts of the world but not love. I can finally feel the realness and meaning of life from being with you all.

"So are you still thinking about leaving India and going back for your work?"

"What can I do? I have taken all the responsibilities for that project. I must go."

"But Amit... I love you so much. How will I live without you?"

"Then you come with me too. You, me and Kaveri Amma... We'll live happily ever after."

"Amit, you know this village needs me. I love this village. I can't be happy anywhere else. Please Amit, don't leave us behind. We all need you too."

"I know Geeta. But I have to go I'm already so acquainted with my lifestyle there. I can't live my whole life here."

"Okay then here's my final decision - I can live alone but I won't leave my country. I don't think you love me."

"That is not true! I love you so much Anushka--"

"Anushka...? Who's this Anushka?" She became angry.

I was totally surprised for few moments.

"Did I say Anushka?" I finally said.

"Oh... No, no, Just forget it." She looked bit tensed. "I think it was my bad, I heard it wrong!"

"No... You heard right. I do know an Anushka. But I can't recall where I know her from."

"Trust me you don't know anyone by that name. May be you heard the name in some movie you may have seen or something." She said with worry in her voice.

"May be..." I moved closer to her and held her hands. "But why are you so tense all of a sudden? Did something happen?"

"No, no. Why do you think that? I'm Okay. I'm just worried that you'll leave us and go back to America"

"I don't have an option dear. Anyway, would you please give going there with me a second thought? I'll call you a few days later." I left. Geeta was all alone.

The next morning I bid goodbye to all the villagers and started my journey back to America. Once I got back I kept reminiscing about Geeta, Kaveri Amma and all the simple souls in the village. I *couldn't concentrate on my work. Somehow after six months I successfully finished the project and we launched the satellite. Immediately after completion of the project I resigned and came back to India. Everyone was so happy to see me back again. I started living a peaceful life in Charanpur. But I still wasn't so happy there as I thought I would be. No matter how much real love I felt from Geeta, and she loved me dearly, I was missing someone. I don't know who. Thus, my new life went on...*

...and then I woke up from the dream. Wow, that was a nice dream. The concept of living as a movie character went really well. Thank God I successfully managed to trick myself when I thought about the name Anushka. Otherwise, I would've ruined my dream again. As I got up from the bed, I looked at the clock. It was eighth in the morning. But I felt so weak. I didn't even have the energy to walk. What had happened to me? Why was I feeling so weak? May be it was the wine that I had drunk lots of the night before. I was incredibly thirsty as well. I went to the kitchen for a glass of water. As I entered the kitchen door I got a whiff of a weird smell. I tried to sniff around literally to find out where it was coming from. It turned out to be the egg curry. It was totally spoilt. I should've kept it in the freezer. But I didn't understand how it got stale so quickly. I kept it outside last night. It was only eight in the morning then. So, how did it go bad in a few hours? I immediately grabbed the sides of the utensil and ran outside. I threw everything into the garbage along with the utensil. Back inside I sprayed room freshener to get rid of the rotten smell.

Suddenly, I realised something - Last night I slept at around three o'clock. I had a long dream. I woke up at eight. Does that mean I had such long dream within just five hours of sleep?! I ran to my bed and picked up my mobile to see the date. I had such a "what the fuck" moment - It was 25th May. I fell asleep on 23rd night. That meant I slept for a whole day and five hours, twenty-nine hours! That's why I was feeling so weak. Oh God... It was the longest sleep of my life. Watching Bollywood movies before dreaming and basing them on it was a really great idea. From that day on I kept doing the same. I went into lengthy bouts of dreaming. One morning, after about a week, I lay in my bed talking to myself inside my head again.

"Amit, it was really beautiful to have dreams based on movie scripts. But I don't know, I really don't seem to be feeling the kind of love that I do for Anushka in real life."

"Yes Amit, You are right. Love seems to be a feeling limited to reality only. It comes directly from the metaphoric 'heart', not from the 'mind'. Since my dreams are being controlled by my mind it can't manifest a real feeling of love"

"Can't I control my dreams through the 'heart'?"

"How would that be possible? Human thinking only originates from the mind. Not from the 'heart'. Only the 'heart' can feel emotions."

"Yes, But those uncontrollable emotions and feelings are technically created by some part of the mind, right? Only after experiencing them do people think that it came from the heart because no one likes to admit that they don't have omnipotence over their own minds. See, in my dreams I'm completely living a real life with both 'mind' and 'heart'. These are not the lucid dreams where the self knows that it's just an unreal dream."

"Hmm... What's the problem then? Why am I not feeling real love?"

"May be my mind is not able to create real feelings in my dreams. May be my memory of Anushka has already created the space which is reserved for true love."

"So, do you think that my mind is unable to create those same feelings for another girl in my dreams?"

"Yes. In real life when I see a girl, whether on the streets or in movies, I might be attracted to her or even fantasize about her. But do I feel the same love for that I feel for Anushka?"

"No. I can't leave Anushka for anyone. I may have flings with them, but if Anushka ever came into my life I wouldn't care about anyone else even if she was the most beautiful girl in the world."

"Exactly... So, if in real life I can't feel love for anyone but Anushka, then how would I in my dreams?"

"True. So, what now...?"

"Anushka... I need to bring her into my dreams. I need to replace the female character as well. I bet that will give me feelings of true love in dreams."

"No! Please Amit. Don't do that. The pain would be unbearable when I'll wake up and find that Anushka is not mine in reality. Please Amit, I'll learn to live without true love in my dreams and enjoy other things. But don't bring her into my dreams!"

"But without love, life is incomplete! You do know why I left my career and sacrificed everything to live this life, right?"

"...To control your dreams so that you may enjoy your life in dreams. All right then be honest here - Suppose Anushka came to you right now and asked you to marry her, will you deny her and say that you are happier in your dreams? Wouldn't you start living real life and forget about living in dreams?"

"Well... Truly speaking, if Anushka came to me I would love to go back to my original life."

"Right... That means you stay here alone and try to live in your dreams only because you lost the love of your life. You think without love life has no value. That's why you sacrificed everything. Whereas, you controlled your dreams only to get rid of nightmares; to sleep peacefully at night; to not waste the eight hours of your daily seeing bad dreams. You didn't do it only to live a different life in dreams to try and forget the truth. You lost Anushka and with that, all colours and tastes from your real life. That's why you're here now."

"So how will it not help if I bring Anushka into my dreams?"

"You still don't understand. The way Amit is incomplete without Anushka in real life, the same way Amit is incomplete without her in his dream life too. If I bring her into my dreams, the only thing lacking in my dream life i.e. real love, I'll get that too. I'll get everything in that life. My dream life will feel even more real, if I have my love there..."

"So, please let me bring Anushka to complete Amit. Without her, Amit is void."

"Yes, I can understand that. But think about my real life too. Wouldn't I be shattered every time I wake up to realize she is not mine in reality? How do I bear that pain every day? Isn't there any alternative way to feel true love in dreams?"

"There is another way. Start loving someone else in real life. If I can really love her as much as Anushka, I'll bring that girl in to my dreams."

"What nonsense! How can I love someone other than Anushka? You know how much I love her. If I could, I wouldn't have left everything and stayed here doing this, would I?"

"Exactly... That's what I'm saying; Amit cannot love anyone else neither in real life nor in dreams. You and I are the same Amit; the same Amit both in real life and in dream life."

"Hmm... But how do I deal with waking life. It's impact on the self will be devastatingly more."

"I know. But think. Nowadays I'm sleeping twenty hours, the whole day, sometimes even more than thirty hours into the next day. But awake only for a few hours. I can live my dreams as real life and my real life as a dream. Just consider the waking hours as just another bad dream where Anushka is not there with me. Sacrifice something to get a good life in my dreams. Think about those long periods where Amit would be living a very nice life in dreams."

"Okay, as you wish. I'll have to bear that pain. But at least I'll be living a much happier life in my dreams... So, what movie shall I watch today?"

"'Tere Naam'..."

"What? No! That was a tragic love story. The heroine dies during the climax and the hero becomes a lunatic."

"So what...? This is my dream. I can change the climax where both will unite and live happily ever after."

I downloaded the movie and watched it completely. As usual while in bed I started imagining the movie with the lead male character replaced by me and the female character by Anushka.

"Wow! Anushka looks superb in this dress."

I kept thinking for hours but did not get sleep. I opened my eyes and sat down on the bed.

"What will I do, I don't feel sleepy. I love imagining Anushka."

"I'm not feeling sleepy because I'm happy so my mind doesn't want to rest. I need to take extra sleeping pills this time."

I took two more and collapsed on the bed. My eyes were about to close but still I started imagining Anushka in that movie. Within a few minutes I went into the dream. I slept for thirty-four hours. When I woke up I didn't feel like getting up but I was hungry.

"That was really a long dream. I can't believe that this is real and that was a dream. At thirty-four hours this seems to be the longest dream of my life. But how did it last so long?"

"Well, I was so happy in my dreams that my mind wasn't allowing me to lose consciousness in my dream and thereby wakeup."

"Yes, that was really a nice dream. It felt so real. For the first time ever I felt the real emotion of love in my dreams. But what could be the reason for such long dreams?"

"Hmm... Remember, when I used to have bad dreams in the past, I would wake up several times in night. I had the shortest dreams at the time because when I got scared in my dreams, my heart rate increased and my mind felt so uneasy that it became too unstable to generate the dream anymore and would wake me up instead. But if the dreams are sweet then the whole body starts enjoying it. My mind, my heart, my whole nervous system tried their best to keep me in that state. So I dreamt longer."

Since then not only did I watch movies and dream about myself, but also about Anushka. They kept getting longer still. In one instance it lasted forty-four hours straight. But at the same time my health started deteriorating. I lost ten kilograms in just a week. I became so weak. One morning I couldn't get up from bed. My head was spinning and I had a high temperature. That particular day my dream lasted for twenty-six hours. I was hungry, I couldn't even walk; I didn't know what to do. I needed a doctor.

I searched on the internet from my bed and got some numbers. I dialled one.

"Hello?"

"Hello, Am I speaking to Dr. Bhat?"

"Yes. Dr. Bhat here..."

"I'm Amit Khanna. I woke up morning feeling so weak that I can't even walk and go outside. I've a high fever too. Can I get an appointment immediately doctor?"

"Well, I'm in my clinic now. If you come by then I'll definitely give you a check-up but I can't leave my clinic open."

"I really would if I could. But it's very serious. I can't even get up from bed. Please it's urgent. If you don't mind I'll pay you the amount that you'll lose for the time you'll be away from the clinic"

"Okay Mr. Amit you certainly made a fair proposition. You hold it together; I will be there as soon as I can. Message me your address."

"Thank you very much doctor. This will not be forgotten any time soon.",

I hung up the phone and sent him my address.

I was still hungry but I knew there was nothing left in the kitchen so I ordered a pizza. It got there within an hour. Somehow I dragged my feet to the door; resting my hands on the walls, furniture and fixtures and using them as crutch. I figured I would've to get up again for the doctor so I pulled a chair next to the door and sat there with the pizza box in my lap. I was so hungry that I finished the large pizza within minutes.

I felt a little better. After sometime the doorbell rang again.

"It must be Dr. Bhat." I opened the door.

"Amit Khanna?" The doctor asked.

"Yes, Dr. Bhat. I'm Amit. Please come inside. And thank you very much for coming down here."

He sat down on a chair beside me and gave me a physical examination, checked my temperature, pressure, pulse, etc.

"That's quite a fever." He said. "Plus you look so thin Amit, your hands are trembling, your body's become so weak. Aren't you eating properly?"

"Well, actually I don't feel hungry too often. So I occasionally skip dinner or lunch."

"But that's bad. I'll prescribe some medicine. Take this regularly; your appetite will be restored. And take that for the fever, thrice daily for two days. If your temperature doesn't fall call me. I'll change your medication."

"Will do, doctor. Should I worry?"

"Well, only a full battery of tests can tell us whether we should worry or not. For now it's just a fever. It can happen due to a lack of protein in your diet. This is temporary and can be reversed. Have your food properly, everything will be fine. Anyway I should leave now. I have to go back to my clinic."

"Thank you very much doctor."

After he left I took one dose of the medicine and rested on the chair. The doctor said I needed to eat in a timely manner. Now, how would I do that if I would be asleep for more than a day's time non-stop? I was in deep trouble. But I knew I take care of my health as well. But I had become so habituated to long periods of sleep; I wasn't sure what to do.

"Yes! I'll use an alarm." Finally I had an idea.

"Such a simple solution... Why didn't it occur to me earlier? You're a genius Amit." I said to myself sarcastically.

"Well, thank you. Thank you." I played along.

Since then, I would set the alarm before going to bed and sleep for ten to twelve hours maximum, at a stretch. After a few days it became frustrating. I wasn't able to finish a single story in my dream. The alarm kept breaking the story half way through. Sometimes I would wake up during romantic situations and I feel so bad after coming back to reality. One day I got fed up...

"This is enough Amit. What's the meaning of stay in dreams if the experience is always incomplete? It would be better to try live in real life then. I should go back to dream randomly as I used to. No story, no logic. I should do something about this. Any suggestions...?"

"Yes. I have an idea."

"What?"

"Take the example of my real life. See, every day I go to sleep then the next morning when I wake up, my life continues from there itself."

"So?"

"Let's say I go to sleep tonight. Today is the 8th of July. When I'll wake up tomorrow it'll be the 9th. So, my real life will pause in between when I'll be sleeping. Tomorrow it'll start right from where I left it today. Simple... Likewise, if my dreams start from the point where I leave them last, it'll continue just like real life. It'll be just like watching a movie in an episodic format daily."

"You mean to say that the moment I wake up from the dream I'll save it somewhere and then when I go to sleep again, I'll start dreaming from that point where I left off."

"Exactly... You can call it 'continuous dreaming'. That means one dream will continue on till I decided it end."

"Wow. So, is this possible?"

"Why not...? If I can dream about anything then why can't I dream from a particular point in time? Instead of watching the movie from beginning to end, I can watch only a portion. I'll be limited to imagining just that part of the movie and dreaming from the beginning till the end of it"

"Okay, but what about memory? Can I remember what I had seen in the last dream? If I can't remember, then starting the dream from half way will seem improbable. Amit won't believe that it's real and will come to know that he is dreaming."

"Oh... I had forgotten about that. Let me think. Can't I have some memory of my dreams? In the real world, we still have the memories of past when we wake up. Sure we sometimes forget something - say for example I sometimes forget that 17th September is my birthday - but if I say to myself that I have to remember this somehow, then a better space for it is created inside my memory. So, I can recall it later. Likewise, if I have a meeting tomorrow, I talk to myself that tomorrow there is an important meeting. Don't miss it. The more I keep repeating this to myself the more probability is there for me to remember. I have to talk to myself about not forgetting that I have to do something tomorrow. Similarly, I would have to remember and restore the whole dream into my memory before going to sleep again. Hmm... I've to create a task in each dream to remember the whole thing by."

"Is it possible?"

"I don't know. I'll start experimenting from today"

"Any particular movie more suited for this?"

"Wait. I have a better idea. I'll live my real life in dreams. The only difference will be that, I'll have Anushka, luck, money, success everything in my dream. I'll start writing the script before I start imagining it. That'll definitely show me the dreams that I want."

"What about the alarm? It can ring at any random moment in my dream. So how would I save the state of the dream before waking up?"

"You forget that I can lucid dream."

"Yes, But in lucid dreaming I'm aware of the dream. I know that it is a dream and not real."

"So? It's still a dream. After I wake up from the dream, I'll close my eyes immediately to induce lucid dreaming and imagine the last situation I was in, in the dream I just had. Then through lucid dreaming I'll make myself think that it's night now and that I should go to sleep. After I make myself sleep in the lucid dream, I'll wake up here in real life. The next day I'll start dreaming from the morning where I wake up from my sleep and my dream life will start from the point where I left it before sleeping. It'll carry all the memory of my life within the dream because it'll be my real life's story just with desirable changes."

"Wow... Theoretically it sounds pretty good. But will it actually work?"

"It may be difficult initially but it is possible. I'll make it work. I know I've complete control over my brain."

"Okay. So, from which point of my real life should I start? Hey, I want Anushka to be in my life from very first day of the dream. Should I start from the day when I met her?"

"Yes. That'll be great. Remember the date; it was September 2nd, 2003 when the new batch entered the college for the first time."

"Cool. Now I only need to remind myself of all the important days in my life till that date to have all my memories in my dream. However, I won't remind myself of anything after that. Otherwise, I'll be able to predict future. That'll make the dream unstable. In my dream I need to change my future just after that point in time. So remember, I only have to remember everything till September 2nd, 2003. If I finish reminding myself and I'm still not sleeping, I have to remind myself again and again till I finally go to sleep and start dreaming."

It was eleven at night. I lay on my bed reminding myself of all the important events in my life since childhood. I started remembering when I went to school for the first time; when my dad brought the big 25 inch big colour TV home and how excited I was as it was the biggest TV in our colony. I remembered the scariest nightmares I had in the past; passing my 10th standard; how my dad punished me when I got 3rd division in 12th standard; how my parents had the accident and died; when I joined college; meeting Saraf; all the hostel raging incidents. I kept recalling all those events again and again and eventually I went into my dream world.

Dream Log:

My friends and I were standing near college gates. There was a long row of juniors coming in one by one. We're all making fun of them by teasing with funny introductions.

"Saraf, do you remember last year we were in this same row? I tried to run and escape but one senior caught me!" I told Saraf.

"Oh Yes. I forgot to thank you then so let me tell you right now - thank you very much." Saraf replied.

"'Thank you'?! Why?"

"Just before you tried to escape, I was thinking of doing the same. But you saved me by being the canary in the coal mine (laughs)!"

"Hey, look at that girl. Isn't she cute?" I changed the subject.

"Who...? The one in red...?" Saraf said while rubber necking.

"What horrible taste you have Saraf! That girl...?! Come on. I'm talking about the girl in the blue suit. Just look at her."

"Oh, that one... She is okay but not that beautiful. I like the red one."

"Fine... You love that red one then."

"Excuse me, Love?! What are you talking about? I'm just saying that the red one is sexier than   any one. Are you telling me that you fell in love with the blue girl on first sight?" Saraf asked with a look of ridicule.

"Don't laugh. I'm not saying I love her. I'm just saying anyone can fall in love with her."

"Anyone...? You have got to be kidding me. How can someone fall in love without getting to know her first?"

"I don't need to know much about her. Look at her eyes. Her eyes in and of itself speaks volumes about her character. And her innocent face... You wouldn't believe me Saraf, but I feel I have seen her somewhere before. I can't recollect. But--"

"Are you losing your mind now too?"

"May be... Only time will tell."

I kept staring at her at length till her turn came.

"Introduce yourself." One of my friends said with heaviness.

"I'm Anushka. I'm from—"

"Hmm... Anushka 'who'? Anushka 'Clinton'?"

There was a cacophony of laughter. She was standing still in the same position. One could smell the fear.

Suddenly it struck my mind "I think I know this name."

"Hey Naveen, You go ahead with the other juniors. I'll take her introduction." I intervened.

"So your name is Anushka?" I asked her.

"Yes Sir." She replied in a scared voice.

"Be comfortable. I'm not sure but I think I have seen you before."

She kept looking down without a reply.

"Your full name is Anushka Patel, right?"

"How did you know?" She asked with surprised look. "Oh, you read it from my identity card" She clutched on to her ID hanging around her neck.

"Maybe or maybe not. I don't know. But I have seen you before. I have heard your name many times in past too. But I can't recall. Where are you from?"

"Gujarat, sir..."

"City...Ahmedabad, right?"

"Yes, Ahmedabad..."

I looked at her for a little bit and said "Okay, You can go now."

"Thank you, sir." She briskly walked away.

I kept looking at her from behind in the hopes of seeing her turn her head towards me. "Yes!" After few seconds she turned and gave a nice smile. "God... Her smile is so sweet." Her smiling gave me the inkling that maybe she liked me too. "Isn't this love at first sight?! I think this is my first love." I thought to myself as I went back to the classrooms.

Niharika Madam was taking C++ class. Saraf and I were back benchers. We never did our homework properly, so we tried to hide ourselves by sitting in the back, just two or three rows from the last row as the last row itself would easily get us noticed by the lecturers.

"What are 'public', 'protected' and 'private' in C++?" Madam asked.

Around ten per cent of the students raised their hands.

"Me Madam, me..." Jimmy requested with a big glee showing his big teeth.

Jimmy, the topper of our class, is the favourite among all teachers and thus an enemy for many of us. He is arrogant and cocky, always finishing the chapters before they are taught in class and always took every chance he could get to answer questions while looking everyone else in the eye with the sole motive of trying to make us feel dumb.

"Yes Jimmy." Madam said.

"'Public', 'protected' and 'private' are three access specifiers in C++. Public data members and member functions are accessible outside the class. Protected data members and member functions are only available to derived classes. But private members are only available to their own class."

"Very good, Jimmy...!"

"Next question... What is an adapter class or a wrapper class?"

Nobody raised their hands.

"That's definitely a tough question." I thought.

Few seconds later, Jimmy stood up, raising his hand and looking at everybody in the class with a smirk on his face.

"All right, Jimmy. You answer."

"It's a class that has no functionality on its own. It's member functions hide the use of a third-party software component or an object with non-compatible interface or a non-object-oriented implementation."

"Excellent. You have a very bright future ahead of you Jimmy. I hope you top again this year. And all of you learn something from Jimmy."

"Thank you, mam."

"Okay. Now let's shake things up. This time you'll raise your hand if you don't know the answer."

"Oh, God... What is this?" I rolled my eyes. "Anyway, I won't raise my hand either way." I told myself.

"What is function overloading and operator overloading?" Madam asked.

I looked throughout the class to see if any one of the students raised his hand in which case I would also raise my hand so as not to standout. But everybody just sat silently as if they knew the answer.

"Hey, you know the answer too?" I whispered to Saraf.

"I don't. Be quiet." He whispered back.

"Who's that? You there, yes you. What you are whispering? Both of you stand up.", Madam indicated with her finger.

Saraf and I got up.

"What is your name?"

"Amit... And this is Saraf."

"Okay, you didn't raise your hands, right? Then give the answer!"

We both remained silent.

"What? Don't you know the answer? Then why didn't you raise your hands?"

"We were just about to raise them before that you asked us to get up." "Shut up! Okay then tell me, what was the question?"

"'Overloading'..."

"What 'overloading'?"

"Overloading in C++?!"

"You guys don't know the question, don't know the answer and still dare to disturb the class? Both of you get out! I'll not mark either of your attendance today."

"Sorry madam. Won't happen again..."

We both requested a lot. But madam would hear none of it. We got out of the class. "Forget about the attendance man. We'll make it up later. Let's go to the hostel. Everybody's probably playing cricket there. We'll join them." Saraf said. We ran to the hostel. It was within a kilometre from our college. There was a small field in front to the hostel and some of my friends and seniors were playing cricket. We joined them and played for a couple of hours till it was five in the evening.

"Hey guys I'm going for tea. Anyone cares to join?" I asked.

Everybody agreed and we went to the tea stall that we usually hung out at every day.

"Wait, here take two rupees. Bring one Flake cigarette for me."
Jeetbhai, one of the seniors told me.

"Okay, bhai." I took money and we went for the tea.

Just then the alarm broke my sleep.

As per plan, I didn't wake up completely. I just turned off the alarm and went back to sleep. I started thinking that I was going to the tea stall. Within moments I was back in my dream but with a conscious mind. I was aware that it was a dream. I was lucid dreaming.

Dream Log:

I turned time faster and did all the necessary things quickly. I finished my tea and bought the cigarette for Jeetbhai. In a few minutes it was ten at night and I finished my dinner. Then I went to the bed. While sleeping I thought about the whole day; about Anushka, whom I had met for first time and wound up falling in love with. Eventually I fell asleep in the dream.

I finished my lucid dream and woke up. All of that happened within just a few minutes of lucid dreaming. It went surprisingly well. I wrote it all down in my diary. It was just like a time machine. I went back to 2003 to correct the mistakes that happened to my life. Tomorrow I must start my dream exactly from that point. I had just slept in my dream. Now I'll wake up the next morning. I finished my lunch and went to the bed for another six hours of sleep. I would wake up at eight in the evening and then after dinner I'll go back to sleep again. I took two tablets of sleeping pills and set the alarm clock to seven hours later. Then I started reading the diary entry where the last dream was written. I closed my eyes and started thinking about it. I imagined that I had just come back from the tea stall, had finished my dinner and was now asleep in my bed. After sometime I went into a deep sleep and started dreaming again.

Dream Log:

I had just woken up to a lovely morning. The clock said eight. Saraf was in front of the computer and eating something.

"Saraf, what's for breakfast today?"

"'Idly'..."

"What? It's Wednesday. 'Idly' again...? Wasn't Today was 'dosa' day?"

"Are you still dreaming or what? Today is Tuesday. Tomorrow is dosa day. Get up soon. We need to go to college early."

"Today is Tuesday?! Huh..."

"Anyway, why so early...? Class is at ten, right?"

"Yes. But today we'll go at nine. You forgot? Today is first day for the juniors. We'll have fun with the juniors. Come, get ready soon." Saraf left the room.

I thought it was strange that it was first day for the juniors again. Perhaps they were students from a different branch. I finished breakfast, got ready for college and went to stand in front of the gates with all my friends.

The juniors formed a long row. All my batch mates were taking introductions one by one as they entered. I had feeling that I had seen this before. Then it struck me. They were the same people from yesterday. I wondered whether I had seen the future last night in my dreams or what. I couldn't make head or tail of it.

"Hey Saraf, you won't believe me but I've seen this in my dream last night."

"What? You mean you know what'll happen in future?" He asked with a sceptical look on his face.

"May be... But really I've seen all of these juniors before. I'm sure it was in my dream."

"(Laughs) now you're pulling my leg! Save that for those juniors."

"I'm serious Saraf. I have seen the future in my dream!"

"But you used to have nightmares? What happened to those bad dreams?"

"I don't know. When I woke up today I couldn't recall my dream. But when I saw these guys here, I remembered that I had encountered this exact same situation before. You don't believe me, right?"

"No and neither would anyone else."

"Okay, look at that girl in red. You have a crush on her. You think she is the sexiest among them all."

"Yes, she is sexy and I do have crush on her. But that doesn't prove anything. It's safe to assume that anybody could have a crush on her. Anyone would say that she is the sexiest girl among them all."

"All right, look at that girl in blue then. According to you she is just okay. Let me call her."

"Hey wait! When did I say that she is just okay? And why are you calling her over?"

"Hello. You, yes you. Come here"

She became more scared because her turn hadn't come yet but she was still called out. With baby steps she came towards me.

"Now see Saraf". "You are Anushka right? Anushka Patel?"

She gave a strange smile and looking at me said,

"Yes Sir. I'm Anushka Patel. Do you know me sir?"

"See Saraf...? How did I know her name? Tell me..."

"Well, I also knew her name is Anushka Patel."

"How...?" I was surprised a little.

"Look at the identity card. 'Anushka Patel'."

"Honestly, I didn't see her ID card. Okay then, I know one more thing. "You are from Gujarat, right? Ahmedabad...? Am I right Anushka?"

"Yes Sir! But how did you...? Do you know me sir?"

"It's nothing. He doesn't know you. He's just good at reading face of people. So, he just guessed it. You can leave now."

"Thank you, sir." Anushka briskly walked to the college.

"What is this Saraf? You still don't believe me?!"

"You're really very smart. You guessed perfectly. But I also know that most of the people having the surname 'Patel' are from Gujarat."

"Fine... Don't believe me then. I'm going to class." And I left.

After sometime both Saraf and I came inside and took our usual seats in the classroom. Then Niharika madam stepped into the mix. "Yes. I've seen this too. Now Saraf will have to believe me..." I said to myself.

"What is 'public', 'protected' and 'private' in C++?" Madam asked.

A few students raised their hands. I did too.

"Mam please...! I'll answer." I stood up and shouted.

"Yes, your name?"

"Amit Khanna, mam."

"Okay. Answer..."

"'Public', 'protected' and 'private' are three access specifiers in C++. Public data members and member functions are accessible outside the class. Protected data members and member functions are only available to derived classes. But private members are only available to their own class."

"Very good, Amit...! I hadn't noticed that you were sincere in my class. Very good!"

I back sat down.

"Wow Amit. When did you study this? I thought you were in my category!" "I told you before; I've seen all this happen in my dream. I knew the question Niharika madam would ask and the answer that Jimmy had given is the same answer that I just gave"

"(Laughs) again you started joking."

"Dude, I'm not joking at all. I know what the next question will be. Just watch."

"Really...? Then tell me oh great psychic!"

"The next question will be – 'what is an adapter class or wrapper class'?"

A few seconds later Niharika madam asked the same question.

"Next question... What is an adaptor class or wrapper class?"

"See Saraf...? Now do you believe me?!" I told Saraf with a glad face.

Saraf was totally taken aback and could not speak a word.

Nobody raised their hand but after a few seconds Jimmy raised his and stood up.

"Please mam." I also raised my hand and shouted.

"All right now Jimmy. We all know you are very good in your studies. Today, let's give this new intelligence a chance."

"Thank you, mam. As for the answer, it's a class that has no functionality on its own. Its member functions hide the use of a third-party software component or an object with non-compatible interface or a non-object-oriented implementation."

The whole class was watching me with looks of surprise scratching their heads.

"Excellent Amit...! That was a very difficult question. You answered it with very simple sentences. You have really a bright future ahead of you." "Thank you, mam." I sat down.

"Okay. Now let's shake things up. This time you'll raise your hand if you don't know the answer."

"Amit, how did you see the future? I still can't believe this!"

"Even I don't know. I think it came from my dream."

"But you get scary dreams, right? So, how did you dream about the future? Is anything bad about to happen?"

"No, no. Nothing bad... I saw that after class we'll both go to hostel and play cricket. That's all. Nothing important... I've seen this whole day pan out man. Remember, in the morning I told you it's Wednesday and where's the 'dosa'? But today is actually Tuesday. So, I have already lived this day in my dream. I should tell this to mam."

"No. She won't believe you." Saraf said holding me down by my hand.

"Don't worry, I'll make her believe. Excuse me, mam. Mam...!" I shouted.

"Yes Amit." Madam turned towards me.

"Actually, I must confess something."

"Sure. Go ahead."

"About the questions you asked just? Well, I didn't know the answer. I have already seen all of this happen before, may be in my dreams. But the answers I gave those were supposed to be given by jimmy."

"What? What are you saying? I don't understand." Madam frowned.

"Actually last night in my dream I saw everything that is going to happen today in real life. I mean I saw the future in my dream. That's why I was able to answer the questions."

The whole classroom started laughing.

"Shut up all of you! Amit... What is this? A joke...? Just moments before, I was commending you. Now you are making fun in the classroom?" Madam said in a harsh voice.

"I'm not trying to be funny at all mam. You can ask Saraf. Before you were about to ask the questions I told him what questions you were going to ask. Saraf please tell the truth!"

"Yes mam. He is right."

"So now the both of you are making fun in this class? What do you think? I'm stupid? Get out of the class. Now...!"

"No Mam. I'm telling you the truth. I even know what that simple question is that you're going to ask now"

"Oh really...? Please go ahead then."

"What is function overloading and operator overloading? That is the question on your mind. Am I correct mam?"

"Okay, are you finished with your joke? Done? Now get out of my class"

"But Mam I guessed the correct question. Why do you still want me to get out of the class?"

"You are wrong. I wasn't going to ask that question. Okay?"

"How...? I saw you asking the same question in my dream... Anyway, what question is on your mind then mam?"

"Nothing... I was going to search a simple question from this book"

"Oh that's why. I should have answered what question after you were done searching for it."

"Now, you both get out of my class or else I'll complain to the principal"

Saraf and I both went outside without arguing anymore.

"Hey Amit... Don't worry. I believe you. But I don't understand how you did see all of these happening?" Saraf said.

"Even I don't know. And for some strange reason I feel like I'm dreaming right now. Wait... wait! Am I dreaming right now Saraf?"

"No. you're not. I'm real. And alive and well..."

"No Saraf! I'm dreaming right now. Yes, that is it! I can fly Saraf. See for yourself" I started flying.

"Wake up Amit. Wake up... This is a dream. Wake... up..."

Thus I woke up from the dream. I shouldn't have known that I was dreaming. This was going to be a really tough task trying to have continuous dream. I should've started my morning in my dream from Wednesday, I dreamt about Tuesday again. I wasn't sure what I should do.

I figured I'll again try to dream from the same Wednesday and I wouldn't write this dream in my diary. I would have to forget it. Otherwise in my dream it'll always stay inside my mind that I can see the future. I should remove this dream from my memory completely.

After that day I tried hard to have continuous dreams. Sometime I succeeded and sometimes I dreamt from a day in the past or a day into the future. I tried for several weeks before I finally achieved it. In some dreams I lived thirty to forty days of my dream life. On rarer occasions I would finished one year of my life in one single session of dreaming. Of course, not only did I speed up time in some cases, but I also skipped the boring days and minutia of life in my dreams. I started writing my own script to be lived out in the dream. I became the topper of my class. I got many more scholarships in my college apart from the one that I was awarded by default for being a meritorious orphan. I became the captain of my college cricket team. Overall, I was the perfect student in my college. Whereas, in my real life I would wake up only for few hours. I would spend my waking life taking my food and medication, going to the bathroom, updating and maintaining my web server, running basic errands for survival and writing my thesis.

December 22nd, 2019.

It was ten in the morning I had just woken up from the dream.

"Finally, today I was able to propose Anushka. She asked me for time to think. Don't worry she'll say 'yes' tomorrow."

"What should I do next in my dream?"

"Umm... First of all Anushka will say a big 'yes' to Amit. Then there will be a long candle light dinner between Amit and Anushka. That's all."

"Only one day's worth of time will progress?"

"Yes. These will be some of the best moments of Amit's life. They should last as long as possible. I'll set the alarm for six hours. I should start writing script. And yes, after this dream Amit will graduate from college and join a big company in Bangalore. One year later, means another dream later Anushka will also join the same company and after few dreams they'll get married."

In this way I started writing the script in real life and making it come true in my dream. Months passed. I had the complete control over my dream. If there was a mistake then I would erase that dream from Amit's mind within the dream. I got married to Anushka. I was the proud father of two kids. I became the CEO of a big multinational company. I wasn't complaining to God anymore as I had everything in my life. I was so happy in my dream life as well as in my real life.

I wasn't even using the alarm to wake up. I became so habituated that when I would go to sleep in my dream life, I would wake up into my real life. That's why I slept in my dreams very rarely, only when my mind told me to wake up in reality. So before going to sleep I would ask myself about the duration of the dream I was going to have and exactly after that duration of time passed in my dream, I would go to sleep in it and wake up to waking life. It became such that my mind could calculate the corresponding real time hours while I was still in the dream.

April 2nd, 2020.

I just woke up from the dream.

"Wow, today Swayambhu started school. He'll be so smart like his father!"

"Amit, I really don't want to wake up daily to face reality."

"But back in the dream, you feel real, right?"

"Yes, But when I wake up sometimes I feel so sad. I know I'll again live the good life in my next dream but... Hey, Amit? Can it be possible to not wake up in real life at all and live in my dream forever?"

"What nonsense are you talking about?! I don't know if that's possible or not. But even if it were, how would the physical body survive? Won't it die after days of no food or water?"

"Yes, I realize that. Don't you have any solution? If someone will take care of my body then I can do it, right?! I have an excellent idea. What if someone takes care of the body just like a coma patient in hospital, won't it be great?!"

"Correct. But coma patients don't wake up to external stimuli like sound or hurt. My dream on the other hand, will be broken if my ear hears any sound or if my body feels tactile sensations."

"Then that'll be my next goal. I'll try not to come out of my dream even if I hear any external noise. I'll try to sleep with the alarm clock. Even if the alarm is set off, I won't wake up from the dream."

"But is that practically possible?"

"Nothing is impossible. All that I've achieved till now was also once impossible. But I did it. I can at least give this a try."

"Okay. So, who'll take care of my body?"

"Saraf... I'll convince him. I know he'll never deny me."

"Hmm... I haven't talked to him in years."

"I know that. But I also know him very well. How about I give him a call right now?"

I dialled Saraf's number. It's been ages since I had last talked to him.

"Hello?"

"Hi Saraf, how are you friend?"

"Hey, Amit..! It's been so many years man... I tried to reach you on your cell phone when you left Bangalore but it was always switched off. Then it went out of service and... you eventually dropped off the planet so to speak."

"Yeah I know. Anyway, this is my new number. I'm in Mumbai now."

"Yes, I heard from your colleagues. So where have you joined now?"

"(Laughs) nowhere friend...! I didn't join any company. I've settled down here."

"What are you talking about? You are not working anywhere?"

"Oh yes I'm. I'm working at trying to live a peaceful life here."

"But how do you manage to live without working? I mean where are you getting money from?"

"I've a steady cash flow from my websites and blogs."

"All right, how much you are making?"

"Around thirty to forty thousand per month…"

"That's too less! How are you managing with that amount in an expensive city like Mumbai?"

"But I'm not in the city! I built a small cottage just outside of town. I got a site at rock bottom prices and now I'm staying there in peace."

"Yet thirty grand is too small to live."

"What is my requirement Saraf?! Two meals a day, some clothes every few months, an internet connection and a meagre electricity bill. I don't need luxury. I buy some vegetables from the market nearby and cook myself."

"Well, aren't you lonely there?"

"Me? Never! I'm sleeping fourteen to sixteen hours a day these days. The waking hours are spent cooking, eating, shitting, shopping, administrating the servers and paying the bills. I'm also writing my thesis in between all that."

"What? Are you finally becoming mad? How can you sleep for sixteen hours? Are you on drugs?"

"Well, I'm taking sleeping pills but they have a come a long since we were kids and are not so harmful anymore. Anyway, I'll message you my address, come by anytime."

"Friend, I'm requesting you again - please don't spoil your life with these dreams! Get back in the workforce, marry a nice girl… your life will be peaceful for real."

"I know Saraf. But I'm enjoying my life as it is too. You once told me that one day you'll be able to feel your dream as if it's real when you sleep. So, here I'm, living a nice life in my dream. I have achieved complete control over my dream. And the best part is my dream has some continuity now."

"Continuity…?"

"Yes, I can see the dream from the point where I left it the previous night."

"Meaning...?"

"See, in real life after you wake up from your sleep, you still retain the same memories of your life from before you went sleep. That means your life starts again from the point where you left it before sleeping. Likewise, I've controlled my mind to an extent where after I wake up I carry all the memories of my dream life. And when I go back to sleep it starts from there."

"Wow... unbelievable. That means you are living another life there in your dreams?"

"'Dreams'?! No 'dreams' my friend. This is the 'Dream'and that is my real life. All along I have a single dream not multiple ones. I have my own memories inside it. When I go to sleep and start dreaming, all my experiences and memories that I've accumulated in past sessions are carried over. The life I'm living in reality seems like a dream in my dream life. That means when I sleep in my dream, I wake up here into my real life. Just like when I sleep in real life, I actually wake up into my dream life."

"This is so unreal. That means you have a different lifestyle in your dream?"

"Yes. In my dream I'm already married with two kids – Swayambhu and Swapna. Swayambhu is four and just started school and Swapna is just turned one. And do you know who my wife is?"

"Anushka...?"

"(Laughs) you're smart Saraf. Yes, Anushka is my wife and my love. And I love her so much. I have such a happy family in my dream."

"Are you telling me the truth? I'm having such a hard time believe all this is possible."

"Trust me on this friend. You're even my best friend in the dream. All the major characters in my dream are from the real world. And I'm a powerful person in my dream. I have everything - money, fame, power."

"But how do age in your dream? I mean your first kid Swayambhu grew up to be four. How did you do that?"

"I write the scripts in real life - when I'll have child, when he'll grow up, when he'll go to school. I write every character's story and make them come true in my dream."

"That sounds great. But I still don't understand how you managed to pull off continuity dreaming."

"That was very tough. At first when I went to sleep, I'd read up on all the things that I'd seen in the last dream. I tried to feel myself into the dream and kept imagining as if I'm in the dream. In spite of hits and misses in the beginning, over the years I was able to start my dream from the previous one. But now I'm master at this. Now I don't even need to think about the previous dream sessions before sleeping. I just need to read the last dream once, go to sleep and I start dreaming from there. I have written everything down in my thesis. By now there are a total of more than two hundred diaries thousand pages each. I have noted down all of my experiments, dreams and theories. It is written in such a way that any person can read it and reach this level, no unnecessary academic styling and jargon. But I don't want others to read these because if everyone started living in their dream world, then the real world will cease to be, civilization will collapse."

"Friend, you are a genius. Once you were the guy who was afraid to go to sleep. But now you are afraid to wake up. I know you are telling the truth, but my mind is having a hard time fathoming this. This is really out of this world. Anyway, are you sure that you're happy there?"

"Yes. Very much so..."

"Can I help you out in any way? If you need any help including financial, please don't feel shy to ask. I'm here to support your dream."

"Right now, I don't need any extra money but I may need your help in other ways. I'm thinking up an experimenting with something. With your help, I can surely get things started."

"Sure, tell me."

"Well, I may not wake up from the dream someday. I intend to sleep forever and live the rest of my life the dream. I don't know when that will happen but if it does can you keep my body somewhere? May be in a hospital? Otherwise I'll die. And I'm not worried about dying really. I mean if my physical body dies here, I'll die in my dream too... So—"

"What the fuck are you saying?"

"I can't explain so much on the phone. I'm just saying, suppose I don't come out of my dream and I'm still be breathing, then would you please take care of my body till I die? Please friend, that's the only help I need."

"I don't want this to happen, man. But if it does, how can I safely keep your body? How can I do this against the law? It'll be illegal!"

"See, if I'm breathing but don't wake up, that means I'm alive, right?"

"Yes."

"And in medical terms, it's called a coma. So, can you fund my stay as a coma patient in any hospital? I don't need a cutting edge place, any ordinary hospital."

"I don't know what to say. Won't anything happen to you?"

"Nothing will happen to me. I'll be still living in my dream life."

"Okay, I'll spend whatever it takes to take care of your body till it dies."

"Please promise me so that I can start this experiment in my dream..."

"But how will I know that you've gone into the dream permanently?"

"That's what I'm wondering about. I'll send you an SMS once every two days. If the SMS's stop, it means my experiment was successful. But first promise me that you'll do it because nobody knows where I'm living right now and my body will die within days. So please promise me friend..."

"Okay, I promise." Saraf said, sobbing.

"Hey, please don't cry. Nothing will happen. I'll lead a peaceful life there. In real life I'll be just a body, but all my emotions, memories, personality will stay in my dream. My 'self' will exist only there."

"Hmm... you take care of yourself Amit."

"You too..."

"Thank God, Saraf agreed to take care of my body. So I should start the experiment from today itself. Come on, you can do it."

I went to the kitchen and prepared a dish. I finished my lunch and went to bed. While I lay there I kept thinking.

"First I'll set the alarm clock then go to sleep. I'll try not to wake up even if the alarm goes off and the sound disturbs me."

I set the alarm for one hour post. By then, I didn't need sleeping pills to sleep. So, I closed my eyes and tried to sleep. I thought about the last dream. Within a few minutes I went deep into sleep and into the dream as well. Usually I went in at the start of every morning. So, I started dreaming from a morning where I woke up.

Dream Log:

I woke up and saw Anushka opening the window screen deliberately trying to make the warm sunlight disturb into opening my eyes. I looked at the clock. It was eight.

"What is this Anushka? It's only eight now!" I said groggily.

"I know. Thank me that I didn't wake you up at seven." She replied with her cute smile.

Seeing her smile always makes me forget all my tension or anger. I got up and sat on the bed.

"Good morning honey. I wake up at nine usually. Why eight today...?"

"You forgot? Swayambhu will go to school at nine. Don't you want to see him before he goes?"

"Oh yeah... My prince started school from yesterday. How quickly the time passes. I feel like it was just yesterday that we got married."

"I know. But it's been seven years since we were married." She jumped onto the bed and hugged me tightly.

"Your breakfast is ready. Get ready soon." She was pulling my hand trying to drag me out of bed.

Suddenly I heard a lot of noise. I was gaining lucidity. I put fingers in to my ears and shouted "I won't wake up. I won't wake up from the dream."

Within moments everything disappeared. I found myself alone sitting in a field where there wasn't even a single bird to be seen. I lay down on the field staring into the blinding sun...

...And I woke up from the dream. My heart was beating so fast and I was sweating. I got up and drank some water.

"I can't Amit. I can't. I tried to stay in the dream but my mind was unable to concentrate. So I couldn't render the sights and sounds."

"Don't lose hope. You can do it. This was just the first attempt. You need to try it again and again till you get it right."

I tried every day not to wake up from the dream at the sound of the alarm but I failed every time. Two weeks passed this way and my dream was stuck at that same morning as I couldn't make it forward due to the failed experiments. One day I lay in bed thinking about my experiment.

"Amit, what can I do? It's not possible for me to remain in the dream with external disturbances. I think I should stop this experimenting and continue as before. My life in the dream is also on hold due to this experiment. Every day I have to dream about the same morning and wake up after the alarm goes off."

"I know. I'm thinking about it."

"What?"

"If I can somehow trick Amit into thinking that the sounds he is hearing are native to the dream and not originating from any external source, then I can stabilize my mind and it won't disturb my daily life in the dream"

"But how do I pull this off?"

"I have an idea. I'll put a real clock in his room so whenever the alarm goes off in reality, it'll start ringing too! Amit will think that the sound is coming from there."

"That sounds good but it won't help me. This is not about the alarm going off. Think. When I'll have gone to sleep forever in real life and the doctors will be taking me to the hospital, I'll hear so much noise - the people talking, vehicle horns, background chatter and much more. It won't sound like the alarm at all. How will I convince Amit then that these sounds are coming from the clock in the dream?"

"It'll all be just noise. When someone talks to me, the sounds will be captured by my ears but it won't render what they are. Our mind renders it and understands the meaning of the sound. When I'm asleep I won't be able to understand as my mind will be unconscious. I won't know what somebody said or if it was a car horn. So any external sound will just be some noise in Amit's dream. I'll only wake up if the noise is loud enough. So, I'll try to convince him that the noise is coming from that clock."

"So, what happens when he switches off the clock but still hears the noise? Or, suppose he is driving and he hears the noise, where will you put the clock? There may be countless circumstances where it'll be very illogical to deal with it this way."

"Yes. Good points. Let me think of something else. How about I make him believe that it's a mental disorder or the symptom of a disease he has where sometimes he'll hear noises? That will convince him, right?"

"Cool. That's a good solution. But is there any disease like this?"

"Who cares? Amit is an engineer, not a doctor. I'll create the disease in the dream which wouldn't be a very unusual disease there at all."

"Nice. So shall I try this now?"

"Wait. Let me search the internet and see if by chance such a disease exists or not. If it does, it'll be so much easier for me to create the script."

I opened the laptop and entered "I hear at times unusual noise in ears." in the search engine. I got so many links. Somewhere it was mentioned that it might happen when some spirit tries to communicate with you! After some searches I found a site where it was mentioned that there's a condition called tinnitus. Its description read:

"Tinnitus is the perception of sound within the human ear in the absence of corresponding external sound. Tinnitus is not a disease, but a condition that can result from a wide range of underlying causes: neurological damage (multiple sclerosis), ear infections, oxidative stress, foreign objects in the ear, nasal allergies that prevent (or induce) fluid drain, wax build-up and exposure to loud sounds."

Great! There already existed a condition which would create noise in my ears. I memorized all of it. I then created a script where I'll wake up in the hospital. I put the alarm at two hours post and slept.

Dream Log:

I was in the hospital when I opened my eyes. Anushka is sitting by the bed holding my hand.

"What happened to me Anushka? How am I here?"

"This morning you lost consciousness and collapsed on the floor. We then took you to the hospital. There is nothing to worry about. You'll be alright."

"But why did I black out suddenly? Where is the doctor?"

"Relax honey. Don't panic. I'm calling doctor." She stepped out of the room.

I used the button on the side to raise the bed and sit myself up. Moments later a bald person came into the room.

(He was actually Dr. Bhat who had once treated me when I had high fever.)

"Hello Mr. Amit... How you are feeling now...?"

"Yes. I'm feeling well. But what happened to me?"

"Well, when you're brought here, you're in an unconscious state. It seems you got some sort of sudden shock which made you senseless. What exactly happened before you lost consciousness? Do you remember anything at all Amit?"

"I don't remember. But what shock? From what...?"

"Try to remember. Your wife was telling me that you were shouting while putting your fingers inside your ears and suddenly fell down on the floor."

I thought a little and said "Oh yes, Noise! So much noise--"

"Noise...? Did you hear some high frequency sound that made you senseless?"

"Yes doctor. I couldn't figure out where the sound was coming from. It felt like someone was shouting loudly into my ears."

"Okay, Got it. This is tinnitus."

"Tinnitus...? What is that?"

"Many people experience an occasional ringing or roaring sound in their ears. That noise doesn't come from your surroundings. Nobody else can hear it but you. This is called tinnitus."

"So, what's the reason behind this? Will that noise come and flood my ears again?"

"Tinnitus is not a disease. It's a condition. There are many reasons for this - ear infections, oxidative stress, foreign objects in the ear, nasal allergies that prevent fluid drain. You need to consult an ENT specialist. I'll refer you one – Dr. Manish Sharma. He is a very good ENT specialist. I'll give you his number. He'll take care of this from now on." Dr. Bhat gave my wife the ENT specialist's number.

"Thank you, doctor. So will this noise come frequently?"

"We can't really be sure in cases like this. It may or may not."

"But will I become senseless every time I'll hear that noise?"

"No, no, Mr. Amit. Many people have this problem. I think this is your first 'attack', so to speak, of tinnitus. The first time you

suddenly heard these noises. That's why you got shocked and lost your sense." "Then how do I deal with this noise? It was so loud."

"Just don't care about it. Whenever you hear it just take it as an external sound coming from a big vehicle or from an alarm clock or whatever is around you. Don't panic, stay cool and calm."

"Okay Doctor. I'll. Can I be discharged now?"

"Yes of course. And don't forget to make an appointment with Dr. Sharma."

"Absolutely... I'll make the appointment as soon as I reach home. Thank you very much for everything doctor."

Anushka and I left the hospital. We got into the car and the driver drove us off being a little more careful than usual. After sometime, while we were in the car I heard the same loud noise again.

"Ashok, stop the car right now!" I shouted at my driver.

He stopped the car by the highway and I quickly got out after fidgeting with the lock for a brief moment. I put my fingers into my ears. I was stabbing them in almost.

"What happened honey?" Anushka held me and moved my hands out of my ears.

"That same noise... It's so loud." I turned away.

"Don't worry dear. Calm down." She held my hand. "Remember what the doctor said. Think of it as a horn of a big truck. Now let's get back in the car and be on our way. Parking by the highway is not safe."

"Anushka, it's too loud" I held my head.

"Don't worry. It won't harm you. It's just a false sound."

Anushka held my hand even tighter... After a few seconds it was over. I relaxed.

"Thank God the noise disappeared." I breathe a sigh of relief.

"But what was the noise anyway?"

"I couldn't understand. I never heard such a noise in my life. It was unimaginably irritating."

After that we went home and had dinner. Anushka asked me to go to sleep early. It was only eight at night. But I closed my eyes and slept fast.

Then I woke up from my sleep in real life.

"Hurray...! The alarm couldn't break my dream! Now I can dream even with any external stimuli. Nobody can wake me up from my dream except myself!"

"But that sound was really irritating. Would I've to go through that all of my dream life or what?"

"Nah... Who will put an alarm near my ear every day? As a coma patient I'll be kept inside a hospital which will be a relatively silent place to begin with. I'll have very few people around me in the hospital who'll be talking. It'll just create the very bare minimum of noise and I can definitely manage to endure that much."

"Cool, then what do I need to do now? Should I meet Dr. Manish Sharma for ear treatment?"

"Yes. But the doctor will say that there is nothing wrong with my ear. This is all psychosomatic and false noise."

I hesitated but decided for it so I went back to sleep again.

Dream Log:

I woke up and looked at the clock. It was half past nine.

"Good morning honey. How are you feeling today?" Anushka asked.

"Good morning sweetie. I'm feeling good. But I slept so much last night. I don't know, I feel like I've become so lazy nowadays." I lamented.

"Oh stop it. You're just unwell yesterday, so you slept more. Anyway, I've already made an appointment with Dr. Sharma. He'll be coming here. You freshen up."

I finished my morning work and had my breakfast. I was at my laptop when the doctor came in.

He pointed a flashlight into my ear and inserted a long soft thread into my ear canal. It had a camera which recorded my inner ear.

"Amit, you don't have any problem with your ears" Dr. Sharma said.

"Really...? Then why am I hearing the noises?" I asked.

"Actually tinnitus happens due to our unstable mind. Stress mostly. You do one thing. Don't pay attention to the noises. After a few days it'll automatically become thinner and thinner and will eventually disappear. Just live your daily life as normal and don't get stressed too much."

"Thank you, doctor. I'll try."

"Oh, one more thing- sometimes you may feel that someone is holding you tightly or you're falling from a height. Those are just a few rare comorbidities/concomitants. So no need to panic when that happens, if ever."

"Okay doctor."

He left and I went back to my office. The rest of the day passed nicely and I went to sleep peacefully.

After that day I set the alarm daily and then went to sleep. Slowly I got habituated with the noise in my dream. It didn't affect my life in the dream anymore. The intensity of the noise gradually started decreasing as I learnt to avoid reacting to it.

Even external tactile activity like touch, push, pressure, pricking on my body didn't wake me up from the dream. In this way a few weeks passed. The time to stay in my dream forever was approaching. I started work on a long script for this.

November 16th, 2020.

I was sitting on the beach near my cottage enjoying the sunset. I tried for several weeks to not wake up from the dream anymore, but I failed every time. The reason was sleeping inside my dream. Whenever I went to sleep in the dream, I would wake up here. Whenever I tried not going to sleep, I felt so tired and sleepy in the dream.

"I'm already much acquainted with staying calm in my dream in spite of external noise or any external activity on my body. But I still can't go to sleep completely. How can I stop Amit from going to sleep in the dream? How?! I can't tell myself this directly as I'll know that I'm dreaming. How do I do it? I need to send somebody into my dream to stop me from sleeping. (Sighs) only God can help me now. Oh Yes! 'God'! God will help me." I started murmuring.

"God...? How...?" Yes. Got an idea.

I have to convince Amit that he is an incarnation of God. He is a divine representative on this earth borne with a specific purpose.

"But who will convince this?"

For this another divine soul should descend on earth in my dream to convince me that I am not a normal human being. I am also a divine soul born for the purpose of saving this earth from so called Rakshasas creating chaos on this earth. Terrorism, rape, murder etc are the activities of these Rakshasas.I have to establish peace and harmony in the society putting all the sins of these Rakshasas to an end.

"OK, done. This is my dream. I can do anything. I'll make Amit believe that he is a divine ambassador from the heaven and has come to earth to save it from destruction by evil powers." – I accepted my own suggestion.

"But how will that help me stay in the dream forever?"

"Cool, let's say another divine soul comes down from heaven and tells you that you are an incarnation of God and are sent to the earth for a specific purpose to be accomplished. He also says that you don't have to sleep at night because you're God and you don't need sleep. You can perform other duties at night. Then will you go to sleep?"

"May be not but how will I manage to live without sleeping?"

"You don't have to. God can live forever without sleeping. He's omnipotent. If I can convince Amit that he is God and he doesn't need any sleep, he won't sleep. And my mind while dreaming is already asleep. So sleeping or resting is not really required in my dream. I was sleeping in the dream because I know it's a daily routine and without sleep my health may break down. But when I'll learn that I'm God, I won't sleep. And if I don't sleep in the dream, I won't wake up to reality and my mission will be successful. I'll live my whole life in my dream. So today I need to concentrate on writing a script for that."

I went back to my cottage and finished dinner. I wrote a short script that would turn me into God. I lay down on my bed and started dreaming.

Dream Log:

I woke up but found that the night wasn't over yet. I switched on the lights. Anushka was deep in sleep. There was no movement in the room. Not even a light breeze. The clock read twenty minutes past three. Strange, the hands had stopped moving. I checked my mobile. It was frozen at the same time "3:20".

"Strange! What happened to all the clocks? All stuck at '3:20'?!"

I tried waking Anushka up. But she wasn't responding as if she was totally unconscious.

"What's going on here...?! Anushka... Anushka!"

Suddenly there was a bright light coming from a corner of the room and I saw someone's silhouette standing there. He walked towards me in slow, heavy steps. I couldn't get a clear view of him as he was surrounded by fumes. After few seconds I could see him. A tall, half bare body with a flower garland around his neck. He had a 'Veena' on his hand. His face was glowing as if rays of light were emanating from the skin.

"Who...? Who are you? How did you get inside?" I screamed out of fear.

"Narayana... Narayana!Deba, don't be afraid. I'm also a divine soul like you." He replied.

"What Deba? I'm no Deba. I'm Amit. Please get out of here!"

"Narayana... Narayana! You're Deba Viswakarma from heaven. Forgot so soon? I'm Narada. Try to identify me. I've come down from heaven. You're a divine soul and you've been born into the earth to save it from sin."

"What? Are you kidding me? I'm Amit and I know I'm a human being. Not any God. I don't even believe in God! I believe in science and it tells me that these all mythologies have no logic at all."

Narada said again politely, "No Deba. God is beyond your materialistic science. We're the scientists of this vast universe and have created the earth, sun, planets, stars, black holes, galaxies, dark matter... The whole of the universe which is actually a multiverse. We've created life. The evolutionary mystery of 'Abiogenesis'? That's us. But this process has led to the birth of evil in some planets. Hence, we periodically sanction rescues. And here on earth, the devil is mankind itself. So, you took birth here as a man to bring peace back to earth. You are Viswakarma. You have constructed Viswa, the earth. Recollect, your date of birth is 17th September, is not it? It's the birth date of Viswakarma. Now your creation is in danger and you are sleeping peacefully? You have no duty to save it?"

Like a mesmerised person I suddenly replied," Yes, I want to save the earth. But I don't believe that I'm Viswakarma. I can reconstruct the earth and establish peace here. You said that the entire universe is created by us. Is there human life in all the planets we made?"

"No. It depends on the planet. There are different kinds of life in all the inhabited planets with different physical laws in a particular region of the multiverse that influences different evolutionary cycles and mechanisms. Some can live in fire, some live floating in the air. All made with different materials that are totally alien to this planet, to this region. To maintain equilibrium in all the planets we go there with different Incarnations."

"So what exactly we are? Don't we die?"

"Different planets' creatures conceptualize us differently and call us by different names. And yes, we never die. Just as in your science 'energy can neither be created nor destroyed'. So, think of us as like we are cosmic energy but with different forms. On this planet humans see us in their human form. Likewise, other planet's creatures see us in their own form."

"Wow... This is so far out. Anyway, how do I know that I'm a devine soul,a part of God? Can you prove this?"

"Look at the time, is that not proof? It's not moving at all because for us there is no concept of time. We move within space-time, we are energy."

"Okay. Let's assume that I'm Viswakarma. Now tell me why have you come here?"

"I'm here to tell you that the time has come. War, terrorism, murder, rape, slavery, corruption... The sins are beyond limit on this planet. You have to bring peace or it'll be destroyed very soon."

"But how...? I'm God sans the extraordinary power to fight evil. I hope, I'm just a normal human here."

"No no, you've the most extraordinary brain which you can utilise. You have lady luck on your side too. But you have to do it all alone. Do you want to see the power of the brain?"

"'Power of the brain'...?"

"Yes. With enough mind power you can do anything. You have such a developed mind. With it you can destroy a world or can create a world too without the physical use of your body."

"Really...?"

"Look at that bronze idol. Now try to melt it. You can."

"Are you joking? I can't melt bronze!"

"Just think of it in your mind and you'll create a high temperature there to melt it. It's all about mind power. Just look at it and imagine hard that it's melting. You have the maximum mind power but you don't know how to use it yet. Now, try."

I then looked at that idol and imagined that it's melting. To my utter surprise, it started melting. I stopped my concentration on it and it did not melt further.

"Unbelievable. That means I can do anything with my mind?"

"Yes. And through this you can motivate anyone. It'll help you in bringing peace on earth. By the way, don't mention this to anyone. Heavenly souls don't talk about the truth to any one on the planet.

"You have opened my eyes Narada. I realise my responsibility now. Unless my objective is fulfilled, I can't sleep now onwards. But tell me, how can I live without sleeping?"

"God never sleep Viswakarma. They don't need sleep.You just go to bed and imagine that it's morning and the sun will rise almost instantaneously. You can speed up time but rest of the planet's creature will feel as if a whole long night has passed. You know, 'relativity' according to your science. Don't sleep. It'll weaken your mind power."

"Okay."

"I'm leaving now Deba. Narayana... Narayana!" He disappeared into the light which shrunk till it vanished.

I stood there shocked, still scratching my head but I was happy too. I looked at the clock it read "3:21", the seconds hand moving.

"Amit... You are a God now. You are lord Viswakarma". "Hurray! I'm from heaven. I'm a God. I can do anything. Yes!"

And with that I woke up. "Congratulations Amit. You've done it. From tomorrow, you'll live in your dream forever."

(Last page) I got up and called Saraf. I reminded him that the scheduled time has come. If I don't send any SMS in the next twenty four hours he should think that I'll have already started living in the dream permanently. Now it was up to him to take care of my body. I messaged him my address again.

The diary ends here.

There was a pin drop silence in the room. Everybody was dissolved in the pages of the diary. It was like a real autobiography. I closed the diary, kept it on the table and said,

"Really a very sad story. What do you think happened next?" I looked up at the others. Everyone was crying. The night had passed and dawn was breaking. Even I felt like doing the same...

"Who can say? The diary is silent about that part..." Rohit broke the silence.

"But why is it incomplete? The rest of the story must be here somewhere." Karthik said.

"Let's search the bookshelf. There are lots of diaries there." Atif said.

Everyone agreed and went towards the bookshelf. There were hundreds of diaries there. On the cover of each there was a sticker with years and dates. I picked up a diary on which it was written "August 2nd, 2005 - October 8th, 2005". I opened the diary and saw some dream logs written sequentially.

"Hey, this diary has dreams written with their dates." I shouted.

"Here also…" Sudheer replied.

"Here too…" Atif shouted back.

"That means these are the diaries mentioned in the diary we just read. Aren't these the thesis mentioned there?" I asked.

"Oh yes. I think so too." Rohit nodded in agreement.

"Let's be sure first. Hey, what day was it when Anushka met Amit at the restaurant and announced her engagement? Let me check that diary." I went through the diary again. "Here it is. 'August 8th, 2007' was when he got the call from the insurance agent. So, Anushka probably met him two or three days later. That would be August 10th or 11th."

We then combed through the dates written on all the diaries.

"Yes, got it. 'July 5th, 2007 – August 16th, 2007'." Rohit pulled it out and sifted through the pages.

"Here it is, the exact dream he mentioned previously. See, it starts from the desert he was walking on." He pointed it out and started reading aloud.

"This is lengthier than what was written in the main diary. It has in so much more details." I said "Look there is some more writing below the dream log with a heading 'Theory'." I started reading it aloud:

"Theory:

Today I learnt that when you lose everything you find that you yourself to be the only person living on the earth. That's why my dream started with me walking alone on the desert. No one was there. I was thirsty. That indicates that when you lose your dear one it feels like the same thirst a person feels when searching for a drop of water in a big hot desert. Which would mean the unconscious mind is not totally devoid of logic. It is more powerful than the conscious mind. With the conscious mind we imagine those things which we have felt or have seen. But the unconscious mind is not tied down like that. It can reach anywhere with its imagination. Our unconscious mind can potentially discover more scientific things which our conscious mind can't even contemplate. With the unconscious mind even a ten year old chap can learn rocket science. But the problem is controlling that mind as it is totally unconscious so you can't really utilise it."

"Now there's another paragraph titled 'Experiment'." I started reading that aloud too:

"Experiment:

Today I went another level up. I can now send any signal to my mind to change the dream. I can play with my dreams. I should now try to bring the things into my dream. Let's say I'm in a jungle and a tiger is running towards me. I'll try to conjure a shotgun in my hand. This way I can bring any person or object into my dreams. This should be my next step. It'll definitely help me control my unconscious mind and I can develop anything using it."

"What a creative theory! Look every dream log is followed by some theories and experiments." I said looking up at the guys.

"Yeah... In this diary too..." Atif said.

"Does that mean it was a real autobiography we just read?" I asked.

"All evidence points to that." Rohit said. "But can it be possible to live another life in a dream?"

"I can't answer that. But that diary was incomplete. It had entries up to November 16th, 2020. That means after that he went into the dream permanently." I said.

"I don't believe it. Maybe he stopped writing. Or he might have met with some accident and died." Rohit retorted.

"Whatever... We should investigate this. It's 2052 so the story is some thirty two years old. It'll be very difficult for us to get to the truth. Anyway, I'll try my best, whether anyone is with me or not."

Everybody agreed to be with me and promised to help in the investigation.

"This is the only house in this area. So, how do we find more information about this place?" Rohit asked.

"I know. Maybe we should try to reach some real estate agent who can help us find the owner's information." I said

"Yes. My uncle works as a real estate agent in Mumbai. If you want we can contact him." Sudheer said.

"Cool, give me his number."

Sudheer gave me a number and I dialled. It started ringing...

"What is his name?" I whispered.

"Uncle Sameer." Sudheer replied.

"Hello...?" A voice from the other side said.

"Hello uncle Sameer?" I replied.

"Yes, Sudheer. Tell me."

" Sory uncle, I'm Sagar, Sudheer's friend."

"Sudheer's friend...? Okay, okay... How can I help you Sagar?"

"I'm extremely sorry to disturb you in early morning but it's urgent." "It's okay 'betta'... Tell me."

"Actually I need owner information of a site in Mumbai. If you don't mind could you find it for me?"

"Which site?"

"It's near Gorai beach. Can you search for one Amit Khanna who bought a site near Gorai beach in Mumbai?"

"Let me search. Hold on for two minutes."

A few minutes later...

"Yes, 'Amit Khanna'. He had bought a site near Gorai beach in 2017."

"Yes, I knew it. I knew that the story is true!" I thought to myself.

"Thank you, uncle. Can you give me his present address or any contact details?"

"Sorry Sagar. There's no more information here. I don't think it's uploaded here."

"Oh... It's okay uncle. Once again, sorry to disturb you...!" I disconnected the call.

"What did uncle say?" Sudheer asked.

"Well, there is no information about him in the directories." I said.

"So what do we do now?" Rohit asked.

"Wait. We can get some information from these diaries. If we can get the name of the college we can get all information from there."

"But nothing hints to the name of his college in the diary."

"The diary we read is not his daily diary. He was writing only the important events in that main diary. I'm talking about the diaries which he maintained daily. He joined college in 2002. So let's start with the diaries with year 2001 or 2002 stickers."

Everybody agreed and we started searching inside those diaries.

"Yes, I got the name of his college. It says here – '...I'm lucky enough that I got admission in one of the reputed colleges in Orissa in spite of my bad rank. Thank God there was a sudden increment in computer science seats in ITER.'" Atif read out.

"Great! That means Amit is from Odisha. We need to search for that address." I said.

"I have my portable gaming device. You browse the internet on it too." Karthik handed it over to me.

I then searched for the college 'ITER Odisha' and got to the official site of the college. We got a few contact numbers. I dialled one.

"Hello..."

"Hello, ITER College?"

"Yes. How can I help you?"

"Actually we need some information about a student who graduated from your college."

"Okay. You're from which company?"

"No, no. I'm not from any company. This is not a verification call. I want the address of a student who passed out in 2006."

"What? 2006?! Sorry, we can't give any personal information about any of our students or staff."

"But... It's urgent--"

She hung up.

"They won't give out any personal information of any student." I said.

"So what now...?" Rohit asked.

"I've got to know everything about Amit. I'll go to Odisha tomorrow."

"What...? How will you suddenly go Odisha?"

"I don't know. I'll go to his college and I'll definitely collect some useful information about Amit."

"Then I'll also come with you."

"Thanks Rohit. We'll both go to Odisha and collect some information about Amit Khanna. We'll share everything with you guys later."

By then the rain had stopped. We went outside the cottage and what a view we had... An immensely peaceful, nice place surrounded by greenery. We couldn't believe that we are standing just outside of a crowded city like Mumbai. It seemed so out of place with what Mumbai is known for. Such a beautiful place!

I booked two plane tickets to the capital of Odisha, Bhubaneswar. The next day we landed there and went straight to ITER College. There was a big gate outside. I imagined that this would be the gate where Amit saw Anushka for the first time. We went into the office and walked up to a young lady sitting in front of a desk. She seemed to be busy with her work on the computer.

"Excuse me, madam." I told her.

"Yes..." She tilted her head up. "May I help you?"

"I want some information about a student who passed out from this college."

"Sorry. We don't share any personal information about our students."

"Please try to understand. We came here all the way from Mumbai only to get some information about someone. It's really urgent." I pleaded.

"But I don't know you... How can I trust you and give you somebody's personal information?"

"Listen to me; we don't need any contact information about a recent graduate. We're talking about someone who passed out in 2006."

"What? 2006?! Why would you need that?" She looked puzzled.

"Actually, he is no more now. He met with an accident last week in Mumbai. He was my teacher. I respect him a lot. I don't know anything about his family as he was living there alone. I only have his college leaving certificate from his room. So we came down here. We need to give this information to his family. Please help us do the right thing; have some faith in humanity; do it out of your goodwill at least." I pretended to cry.

"Oh I'm Sorry. I'll give you whatever information we have."

"Thank you very much madam." I wiped my eyes. "His name is Amit Khanna, 2006 pass out."

She searched on the computer.

"Yes. Here's his profile. We don't have any contact number but yes, we have his hometown address. It's a village called Harabhanga. Note down the complete address."

We took the address and hired a car for the journey. The village was a couple of hundred kilometres from Bhubaneswar. Finally, we got there. It was a very big old house. We knocked at the door. An old man, maybe in his 60s, came out.

"Yes...?" The old man asked.

"Hi, I'm Sagar and this is Rohit. We have come from Mumbai."

"Mumbai...?!" He went back in.

He walked away with as fast a gait as his aging body would allow. He then put out a peculiar type of rope bed thing for us to sit. First time in my life I saw such bed – a wooden bed with coir and jute ropes for stringing instead of a regular mattress.

"Yes, please do tell." The old man said.

"We're looking for Amit Khanna. Do you know where he stays?" I said.

"Amitbhai...? How do you know him?"

"Actually, we've some work with him. Do you know where he is now?" Rohit asked.

"I'm his cousin. Years ago I got a call from one of his friend. After that I don't know anything."

"Which friend and what was the call about?" I asked.

"I don't remember his name. But he asked me for information regarding his family."

"Okay. So, where does his family stay?"

"What family? He doesn't have any family. His parents met with an accident and passed away when he was 14. After that I never met him in person either. We only ever talked over the phone, that also once a year."

"Oh... So sad... Anyway, do you know where he is now? Anything at all...? Please let us know!" Rohit said.

"Yes, his friend told me that Amitbhai had an accident and not to worry much. He is alright now. He had admitted him in a hospital."

"So, did you go to see him?" I asked.

"No. Where from I get the money to go to Mumbai? I couldn't go."

"Do you remember which hospital he was admitted in?"

"Yes, give me a minute... Let me think. The name was in the *'Ramayana'*... What is it... What is it..."

"In the *'Ramayana'*...?" Rohit chimed in.

"Yes, you know that plant's name that heals anything. Hanuman carried a mountain full of that. I've the name floating in my head somewhere but I just can't put it to my tongue." The old man looked at as for hints.

Rohit and I both stared at each other's faces with curious looks.

"Yes...! *'Sanjivani'*... The hospital's name is Sanjivani."

"Sanjivani hospital...?" I sat up. "That's one of the most reputed hospitals in all of Mumbai. Thank you very much uncle. Thank so much."

"I told you." Rohit said on the way back. "He must've met an accident and died. That's why he couldn't complete the diary."

"Yes, maybe or maybe not. We should find the truth. Anyway, they must have a record of him in the hospital. At least we can get some more information there."

We flew back to Mumbai. I got everyone up to speed and we reached Sanjivani hospital. We then went inside and walked as fast as we could to the receptionist sitting there without making it seem like an emergency.

"Excuse me..." I said.

"Yes? How can I help you sir?"

"Actually, we need some information about a patient who was admitted in this hospital."

"Okay, when?"

"Well, he was admitted many years ago."

"Which year...?"

"2020."

"Sorry sir, I don't have access to such old records. You may contact the administrative officers of Sanjivani."

"Where should we go then?"

"The office is on the first floor. It's the first room on the left from the stairs."

"Thank you."

We went to the office room. I asked someone there,

"Excuse me; can we meet any administrative officers here?" I asked a person walking by.

"What do you need?" The person asked back.

"Well, I need to get some information about a patient who was admitted many years ago"

"Okay, go meet the manager. He sits in next room"

"Thank You"

We moved to the next room. An old man with grey hair was sitting behind a large desk busy signing some papers.

"Excuse me sir."

"Yes?"

"We need some information about a patient who was admitted here many years ago."

"You can collect that information from the receptionist on the ground floor."

"But we just talked to her! She doesn't have any access to patient records that old. She asked me to meet you."

"Okay. Tell me, when he was admitted?"

"He was admitted here in 2020—"

"2020...?"

"Yes Sir."

"Why do you need this information?"

"Actually, we're writing an article as part of our college project. That person may be able to help us. If we could just get his present address or anything, it'll be immensely helpful to us." Rohit intervened.

"What article? And how is that person going to help you? You are asking about someone who once admitted here three decades ago!"

"Yes, you see we found an unknown diary in an old house. After reading it we got his alma mater which led us to his cousin brother. He too didn't have any contact with this person. But he told us that in 2020 he got a call from a guy who informed him that this person was admitted in Sanjivani hospital. So now we are here." Rohit said.

"All right... So, what information may I give you? There are lots of patients coming in daily and you're asking me about someone who was admitted in 2020!"

"But sir, there is a database with some record of the patients who have been admitted here right?" I said.

"Yes... But I'm not sure whether we have such old records or not. Do you know his name?"

"Yes, Amit Khanna—"

"What...?! Mr. Amit Khanna??" He shouted.

We all looked at each other with astonished faces.

"Are you sure you have his diary?"

"Why sir...? What happened?"

"He is in our extended care unit right now as we speak."

"That means? He's been here in the hospital since 2020?"

"I'm afraid so"

We all were shocked.

"Why? What happened to him? Why has he been kept here for so many years?"

"He was in a coma ever since he was admitted here. We tried everything but his condition didn't improve. We don't have any hope that he'll come out from that state. So we stopped all treatment and moved him to our extended care unit."

"Coma...?"

"Yes. . . All my life in the medical business, I've never come across any patient being in a coma for more than thirty two years."

"Can we see him?"

"He is totally unconscious. And no one is allowed to meet him. Sorry, He is not in a state to help you in anyway."

"Okay. May I know if he has any relatives?"

"No, I don't think so."

"But this is a private hospital, right?"

"Yes…"

"So, why is the hospital bearing all the expenses for an unknown patient?"

"No, we aren't bearing any cost. We're getting all the funds for him from a charitable trust."

"Why is a charitable trust spending so much for an unknown person? May we know the name of charity?"

"Sure, let me check." He searched something on his computer. "Yes, it's the Saraf Foundation and the owner is one Mr. Amit Saraf."

There was a pin drop silence in the room for a few seconds. We're all speechless. We couldn't believe that the story is completely true.

"What happened?"

"Well, can we please get the address of Mr. Saraf?"

"Sorry, we don't share any personal information about a non-patient."

Everybody started requesting the manager but he was not to be convinced. I didn't have any other choice but to show him the diary.

"Sir, will you please read this, so that you can believe us?"

"This is too long for me to read. I don't have the time. What does it say? Give me a briefing."

I showed him some text from the diary about how Amit Saraf and Amit Khanna are both friends. Finally after some more conversations, the manager agreed to give us the address. We all thanked the manager and asked for his permission to leave. Without wasting anytime, we headed for Mr. Amit Saraf's house. We reached what was a huge mansion with a big garden as the front yard of the house.

"He seems to be a rich person" I said.

"Yes. In Mumbai prime real estate like is exorbitantly costly" Karthik said.

We tried to enter the gate but it was closed. There was a vintage intercom. I pressed the button and spoke into the mic.

"Hello, anyone there?"

"Who are you?" the voice from the speaker said.

"We have some urgent work with Mr. Saraf" I replied.

"But I don't know you."

"No, you don't know us. But we need to talk about Mr. Amit Khanna who is in a coma and resting in Sanjivani hospital."

"Oh, you're from Sanjivani hospital... Please come in."

The gate opened automatically and we went inside. We saw a middle aged man coming towards us.

"Actually, we want to meet Mr. Saraf."

"Yes, tell me. I'm Saraf."

He didn't look too old to be Amit Saraf so I figured he must be the son.

"We want to meet Mr. Amit Saraf."

"Oh... Dad!"

"Yes, your father Mr. Amit Saraf..."

"Well he is no more now. He passed away two years back."

"What...?! Oh, we're so sorry!"

"It's okay. I'm Puneet Saraf. Please tell if I can be of any help to you guys."

"Well, we want to know more about Mr. Amit Khanna."

"Oh, okay. Khanna uncle was my dad's best friend. I remember, when I was a child, he had come to our home once. After that I never met him except at the hospital. My dad made me promise that when he dies, it'll be my responsibility to take care of Khanna uncle. So once a month I definitely go to see him and check whether his body is kept under proper care or not."

"Hmm... We also want to share something with you."

"What?"

"He's not in coma. You probably won't believe me, but asleep. He's been in a dream for thirty two years. He's living a whole another life in there."

"(Laughs) so funny...! I think you guys have been reading too much science fiction and are concocting your own story here."

"No, no. We are not just saying that. If you have sometime, would you mind reading this diary?"

"What's in there?"

"This is the autobiography of Mr. Amit Khanna."

"What? Really?! How did you get this?"

"That is a long story. I'll tell you later. Please you take this and read it completely."

"Okay, I'll read this tonight. Things have suddenly turned so interesting! I met Khanna uncle so many times, but in a mute state. At least I can feel his voice through this diary. I'll return this to you tomorrow. Thank you so much for this. By the way, May I have your contact number?"

"Sure. Please note it down."

We both then exchanged our contact numbers and the guys and I left Mr. Puneet's place. That night I got a call.

The mobile ringing woke me up. I looked at the clock and thought "It's one o'clock. Who could be calling me at this God forsaken hour?" I put my glasses on and waited a few seconds for eyes to get used to the bright screen after being in complete darkness. It was Puneet Saraf.

"Yes, Puneet Sir."

"Oh, I'm so sorry to disturb you at this time of the night. But I couldn't resist myself."

"No problem sir, please go ahead. Tell me."

"Yes, I believe you. I just finished his diary right now. And I'm sure he is in his dream as we speak. I read all the dialogues with my dad. My dad's really used to speak like that. The diction is unmistakable."

"I believe so too. So, what do we do now?"

"Please meet me at Sanjivani hospital tomorrow morning. We'll discuss it there."

"Sure, at what time?"

"Umm... Be there by ten o'clock."

"Okay then, good night."

"Good night."

The next day morning I called up everyone and reached the hospital at ten sharp. We saw Puneet sir waiting for us there. He signalled us over to him and we then took the elevator to the extended care unit of the hospital. We saw Amit sir first time ever, lying on a bed. There was very nice atmosphere in the room. I looked into Amit sir's face. I could feel the joy on his face. We then headed to an office. A gentleman was sitting there. Puneet Sir went over to him and shook his hands. He referred to him as Dr. Saxena. He then proceeded to tell everything about the diary to the doctor. At first he didn't seem to believe it but after he read some chapters from the diary the look on his face completely changed. He was really astonished.

"So, what should we do now?" Puneet asked.

"It'll be such huge milestone in Medical science if we can prove that he has been in a dream for over three decades." Dr. Saxena replied.

"Excuse me, sorry to interrupt, I actually have all of the thesis and theories that were written by Amit Sir. That may help." I said.

"That is really good. We need them. But before that we have to know for sure that he is really in his dream life and not just in an unconscious state." The doctor said.

"How can we know the real truth?" Puneet asked.

"I have one solution but it'll be too expensive."

"What is it?"

"Medical science has come really far. We've a piece of technology called *'REM Capture'*. This is a type of experiment we do with people who have bad dreams. And we formulate a course of treatment accordingly."

"Can you elaborate a little?"

"This is a technology that enables us to see another human being's dream and record it. With this we can capture exactly what Amit Khanna is seeing in his dream."

"How it is possible doctor?" I asked with ardent curiosity. "I've never heard of such a device before!"

"It is very much possible. It normally reads the various signals sent by the neurons in the various regions and lobes of the brain. It tries to interpret the signals, sketch a picture and record it. This is not hundred per cent accurate but still it renders the pictures in such a manner that we can see it. A Lot of research has been going on over the years on this technology."

"That's really nice. Can we conduct an experiment on uncle Khanna's mind with this device?" Puneet asked.

"We can but as I said it'll be too expensive. We don't have such equipment here. And there are very few doctors who actually know how to operate it on a human mind."

"I don't care about money. I'll spend as much as it requires. You please arrange everything and make the appointments with the doctors for this."

"Okay, I'll let you know when we'll do the operation."

"Operation...?" Puneet was startled.

"Relax... It's not a surgical operation. We'll connect some wireless transistors to the external parts of his head."

"Phew! Okay, we'll be leaving then."

A month goes by and I got a call from Puneet Sir. He asked me to come over to Sanjivani as the operation is scheduled two days later. I let everybody know and we all reached there on the day of the operation.

I saw a few doctors putting some white stickers on different parts of Amit Sir's head. They connected a portable device with a screen to the base of the bed on a manoeuvrable arm.

"Welcome guys! We're going to start the *'REM Capture'* system in a few moments." Dr. Saxena directed us into the room.

"I have a question, sir." I said.

"Yes, ask away."

"In which view are we going to see the video. I mean will we see Amit sir's face or can we move around among the different places in his dream?"

"We won't see anything except for what Mr. Amit will see. It'll be something like a first-person computer game. So, we won't see his face. But of course, we'll see everything he is seeing."

I still couldn't believe it but some pictures started to appear on the screen. There were some glitches and artefacts but after sometime it cleared up.

"Oh my God... This is the real dream of Amit sir we're seeing live!"

Dream Video:

There was a big hall with hundreds of VIP's. Everybody wore the same coloured suits. All the faces were similar to each other. Not exactly, but the facial features were. They could still be distinguished from one another. They were all discussing among themselves. We couldn't hear what they were saying but the cacophony was audible. Amit sir was standing there on a big stage and we're only able to see his hands.

"Excuse me gentlemen, shall we start the meeting?" Amit announced. All stopped talking.

"Okay, what's the current population?"

"It's twelve billion now." One guy stood up and answered. *"This year we have a projected growth of 1.6%."*

"Okay. Mr. Hofer, do we have enough space in our cities and villages?"

"Yes Mr. President." Another guy among them must be Mr. Hofer, replied. *"But it'll start to get polluted in two more years at that growth rate."*

"Oh... Then we should build more cities. Mr. Diaz, start construction plans on two hundred new cities and hundred new villages. Complete them in a year. And yes, ask all the reputed industries to build their offices manufacturing units there and start creating job opportunities. Our Government will give them all the support to expand their business. And provide equal opportunities and subsidies to smaller industries as well."

"Okay sir." Mr. Diaz replied.

"Mr. Sharma, give me a brief overview of our world now? What's the status of the living conditions of normal citizens?"
"Excellent, sir... Zero starvation, zero crime, zero poverty. All are leading a peaceful life here, a luxurious life." Mr Sharma replied jubilantly.

"That's good. What about the terrorist activities we faced earlier years?"

"That is totally under control. We have the improved GPS system to track terrorist rebel activities. Everybody is now supporting the current government system. So there is very low probability of any terrorist activities in the coming days."

"Outstanding. Thank you, gentlemen for joining this session. Please submit your annual reports to Ms. Renuka."

He left that hall and went to the balcony of the hundred storey skyscraper. We saw the whole city from there. It was so beautiful. Everything was perfect. After a few minutes, he left the place and went to a gorgeous red car. There were a driver and two white *cars were there too, one in front of the red one and other in the back. He got into the car and drove off with the two white cars following him in a convoy. May be those were security cars for the president. Amit sir was looking out through the window and enjoying the beautiful cityscape that passed. The city was constructed in such a way that there was no traffic jam even if there were lots of vehicles on the road. There were big flyovers all around. So, there were multiple paths to a single destination. After sometime he slowed down at a huge mansion. The gates opened automatically and the car went in. Amit Sir stepped out of the car. It was a very beautiful house. He walked towards the door that ajar automatically and a cute girl rushed into his arms. She hugged Amit sir, looking very glad and said "Papa".*

(To be continued...)